To: Heath~

D1463156

"Take
a
Wicked
Walk
in
the
Woods"

#10

Ancient creatures roamed the Appalachians for centuries eventually executed and enslaved by the human invaders. What remains of the green race is used for sport by the elite in the most secret game on Earth. Decades of evolution and enhancement has turned the mindless beasts into cunning creatures. Hidden away in the thick West Virginian forest by a wealthy madman, the beasts yearn for freedom. Freedom to live wild in the shadows of mountains, freedom to feast once again on human flesh. The 100th Goblin Gauntlet could finally be the time for the world to see monsters again.

GOBLINS

LANCE W. REEDINGER

For sales and/or event appearances, address the author at lancereedinger@yahoo.com.

Book layout and design by Boutique 41 Publishing - www.boutique41publishing.org.

Manufactured in the United States of Ameica

10 9 8 7 6 5 4 3 2 1

Reedinger, Lance W.,
  GOBLINS

III - MATCH

Dawn Before The Storm

Arrival

Training Day

Hallows Eve

100th Goblin Gauntlet

November Pain

I

GAME

1

"My dearest brother David,

"It appears the luck of our land has finally crossed the vast ocean as we did five years earlier. I cursed you not a month ago for taking me to this forsaken land full of ignorant slobs. The war came to my doorstep and I fled into the mountains with the other immigrants, taking only the little coin I've collected in search for your sacred dirt gold. Chasing you around the Irish hills prepared me to be able to avoid and wait out the battles between the American brothers. As the grey and blue soldiers drew closer, I fled deeper into the forest.

"Upon my second week in hiding, I went out of the pan and into the fire as I was captured by the red people. For a day and night, I was bound and blindfolded, hurried up a giant mountainside with only the sound of their heathen chattering keeping me alert. When my blindfold was finally removed, I sat in an exotic tent and their women brought me good meat. A young lad entered when I had my fill. Speaking the proper tongue, he explained that I would be given a chance at freedom

and fortune if I could emerge victorious in a contest. No further explanation was given but the solemn look on the boy's face showed the odds to be heavily against me. No longer bound, as the depth and darkness of the deep woods were all the savages needed to keep me at bay, I watched them train and hunt with arrow and ax. Visions of going into a contest with one of these warriors only made me look to the heavens and tell mother that I would see her soon. A full moon peaked on my third day with them and the lad woke me at the witching hour. He brought me a great feast and canister of good whiskey. While I indulged in my treat, the boy broke down the rules of the contest. Should I be able to return to camp, a great reward would be waiting for me along with my freedom. Begging him for more information, the boy only looked thru my eyes as if I was already a ghost. He told me I was just heading for a scrap.

"A giant warrior awaited me outside the tent and slipped a blindfold over my eyes again, lifting me onto a large stallion with far too much ease. The giant man mounted in front of me and we took off into the black night. After what seemed an age, we came to a sudden halt. I was dismounted and had my blinders removed. The October moon illuminated the area, a forty-meter clear circle surrounded by thick mountain maples. A large dagger and even larger

axe were given to me by the warrior, not an ounce of fear in his eyes as he handed me two weapons while he stood bare handed. 'Make way back if you can,' the Indian sprouted with zero confidence in his tone.

"Seeing mother Ireland fade from sight from the bow of the ship was the first time I experienced fear, when I herd the gurgling snarls from the darkness of the forest a new feeling unknown to me settled in. Dread, dread flowed thru my slender pale frame. I will dispose of the true descriptive adjectives of this event as you will think I've gone mad, but they came at me. Two at first, wild green creatures with eyes yellow like the high noon sun. My time with the Union boys paid off as I remembered some training and backed quickly to a large tree to cut down their numerical advantage.

"Fierce and furious they charged ready to devour my soul. For all the horror of their appearance, these were no proper fighters. Clumsy and frantic were their initial blows thrown at me. My dagger found the throat of one and the axe cracked the skull of the other. Shrieks came from both, the dagger stuck in the one monster's neck as it slunk to its death. My axe got stuck in the thick skull of the other as it staggered away from me, yelling and confused. Confidence and rage swallowed my dread as I gathered my dagger from the now dead green corpse and went after the second ghoul.

GOBLINS

"Growling filled the autumn air and a third, much larger, fiend of the night came at me. The first two stood only to my chest level. This one was a shade taller than I and had a belly as big as the fat man we saw at the carnival back in Kilmrock. By the grace of the good Lord, the clumsy creature stumbled and fell right before me. I gave it a swift boot to the side of its hideous head and brought my dagger down through the back of its pudgy neck. A geyser of red and yellowish blood sprouted from the now howling beast as I shoved the sharp Indian blade deep into its chest cavity from behind. Once the fat thing stopped wiggling, I removed the dagger and stood as a victorious god. My eyes set upon the last standing creature, still staggering around dazed with the axe buried in the side of its head. I charged and another blessing rang down from the lord as the foul fiend finally fell from the wound. A new shriek came from the forest again, knocking my confidence down, but this was no war cry from a monster from hell. The hooting was the distinct yell of the red man as he came flying into the makeshift fighting pit. His giant smile of disbelief sent me into a fit of laughter, surely this was a celebratory cry signaling my victory.

"I am now five kilometers north of what they call Harpers Ferry, deep in the Appalachian forest. The Iroquois have given me their land for the great *victory as they head west to join their tribe to try and fight off total extinction. My warrior rider showed me rivers of that black gold you so desire, buried deep in and below the mountains. I've wrangled a few other Irishmen to help and a few of the freed slaves, we quickly built a nice camp far away from seeing eyes. Honest men who do honest work. Every week a few take off, the tales in town of the green creatures that roam the mountain forest and the sounds at night that accompany them, make even the hardest of these men sleep with their weapons at night. Gather Mary and Junior quickly and make pace to me, we will assemble a force to rid the area of these monsters as our fathers did of the English back home. This coal gold you've rambled about should turn our fortunes for a lifetime.*

Your Beloved Brother,
Lionel Leary
December 1,
1863

"As well, leave the dego girl back in that wretched city. We will find you a proper woman from our new home here."

2

Winter knew she made the right choice, now resting on mother earth staring up at the crystal black October sky. A half moon burst thru the darkness like a white flame. She came here to connect with the planet, not pound dark ale with hillbillies and yuppies with thousand dollar back packs who set out to rough it on the trail. Winter timed her trek to perfection, halfway thru her journey and enjoying October just north of the spooky timeless town of Harpers Ferry. The solitude of the evening was a blessing, a welcomed break from the bearded boys looking for a snuggle buddy with the cute girl with white dyed hair. Deafening silence erupted thru the woods and surprised the beauty, not even the scattering of the smaller forest creatures cracked the air. Winter grabbed her phone from her pack and put her plugs in to enhance the already fantastic atmosphere. Epic fantasy music pulsed through her eardrums.

Beyond the prison compound for the first time, the green creatures sprinted through the unknown forest with speed and enthusiasm, their pointed wicked tails moving with a sinister sway. Not a clue where to go or what to do, only their primal instincts to flee and eat drove their stubby legs. A scent caught the elder of the two and stopped it dead midflight. Meat, fresh sweet meat, not far off. Quickly turning to the left the green ghoul made haste to the scent, his smaller companion following in stride. A human lay still not thirty yards away, the creature's eyes exploded at the sight of the sweet treat. No gun, sword, or whip accompanied the human. Winter would have heard their war cry of glee if she did not have her plugs in, which would have only delayed the feast.

Shaking her bare feet in tune with the sound of the instrumental beats, Winter was in natural heaven. Heaven turned to hell in a quick green flash. Pressure arose on her shoulders and two thin hands pinned her to mother earth. Before she could react, another assailant mounted her around the hips. Winter's eyes reflected a hideous green elf like creature hovering over her. She began to sing a death shriek, but the song was cut short as the fiend chomped down on her soft open throat. Blood and life fled Winter's neck and just as she began her ascent to the stars, two gun blast rang from the woods. Both monster's heads exploded simultaneously. Maybe a night on the town wouldn't have been so bad the young nature princess thought, before she returned to the soft soil for good.

"Status?" Rex radioed to the team, no digital contact on game night.

"Clusterfuck, the greenies got a girl. Looks isolated, everyone down at the town for the festival," one of the grunts responded.

"Thank fuck for that. What we bloody looking at? Loner, hippie, homeless?" Rex questioned, hoping for the last of the three.

"Nope, we got an iPhone and one of those fancy yuppie coffee mugs. Looks like someone is going to be missing her," the grunt answered.

Rex quickly ran through his mental playbook, hippies and homeless throw in the river, locals and kids burn quickly. Anyone worth a damn had to be animal attack.

"Clean up quick, get her two miles north and bring in one of the black bears, be sure to fucking match the wounds this time," Rex bellowed, annoyed with the unwanted distraction.

He dug into the back of his shaved bald head, an awful old habit becoming far more frequent and aggressive over the last year. The shit is definitely getting out of control he thought to himself. Escapes happened on occasion through the last nine years, now five in the last six months and this one on game night. All of his advice and that of his colleagues had fallen on fat deaf ears. He peered down from the top of the tower at the farm. Increased numbers, physical stimulus testing and agitation tactics were just the beginning of the madness being brought down from the big man. Luxury buses began to turn down the perfect concrete path heading to the main gate and the greenies, almost sensing the cargo, began to screech in anticipation. This whole thing is going to end badly one day, but not on his watch. Rex exhaled, bolstering the last of his mental fortitude for the night. After tonight, one more year and the contract would be over. Then he would be back to Sydney for surf, sun, and sheilas. The hard Aussie looked to the heavens, but he did not know why. One thing this job had shown him without a doubt, there is no God.

3

Vanessa Vorner gazed blankly into the decadent wall length mirror. Her dragon green eyes slunk to the hideous scar falling from her shoulder to elbow. Nearly faded to skin tone through the years, it still stung in the West Virginian winters. Water filled her eyes as the visions from that night flooded back. The now powerful woman shook her head to remove the tears and the memory that brought them on. Another glance at the glass and there she was, a fierce woman warrior had replaced a scared little girl in the reflection.

"Loch, the guest are coming, time to get the big man," one of the staff shouted from the other side of her locked door.

Grabbing her neon green power suit off the armoire, Vanessa threw it over her fit frame and made way to exit the lavish room. She made her way down the long hallway followed by two armed minions. They both halted twenty yards from the giant steel door right on silent command and faced the opposite side of the hall as Vanessa headed over to the electronic keypad lock. She gently placed her hand on the blank screen and an immediate access granted response appeared over her index finger. The steel door slid from left to right and Vanessa entered the boss's lair.

Three thousand feet of gaudy decor engulfed her as she started her search for the big man. A small mist coming from the side hall of the giant penthouse alerted her to his location. Walking through the mist and the now heavier fog, Vanessa made her way to the bathroom area. A thick steam cloud poured out of the bathroom as she opened the door and entered. The horrors of the last fifteen years should have made her numb to any sight, but the vision before her made her gag. Six foot four, four hundred pounds of gluttony stood in the middle of the massive shower. Two of the dozen whores he kept at the compound were on their knees, one behind and the other in front of him, both having an evening snack.

"Our guest are here boss!" Vanessa shouted, fighting off the vile fluids shooting from the pit of her stomach. The giant man turned his bloated head toward her and nodded, a sinister grin accompanying the nod.

Vanessa nearly sprinted from the bath house and made her way to the bar area. Staying stone sober on game night was an unbreakable rule, but she desperately needed a shot to wipe that image from her sight and steady her upset tummy. Grabbing the closest tequila bottle and gold platted shot glass, she poured a quick drink and shot it with haste. The light weight of the bottle suggested the big man had been hitting the stuff more than usual, a quick glance at the rest of the expansive bar confirmed her suspicion. It was all getting so out of hand, the monsters, the drinking, the eating, the fucking. Ever since the youngest went off to boarding school in Zurich, the Sixth nearly spent all of his time here at the compound, making a rare stop at the family estate in Charleston. The Leary empire reached the economic stratosphere decades before when the Fourth came into power. Expanding from just cole, to pharmaceuticals, to robotics, and dancing the political two step to perfection. Donating to both sides to secure true freedom and gain the luxury of immunity. Two presidents and countless heads of states have attended the games. By the time the Sixth came to the throne, the Leary empire were quietly the top one hundred richest dynasties in the world. The Sixth being an only child had one job, to breed. Six children, five males, all thru surrogates secured the bloodline. With teams running the empire and no elder family members to answer to, the Sixth was always a greed filled gluttonous monster. Now, with no children to watch over or public appearances to make, he was becoming a truly mad overlord. The games were the one thing that set the family apart and unique even in the diabolical one percenter world, but the Sixth was always obsessed and fascinated with the event. He just passed for the second year on bringing the Seventh into the fold of the games, four years past due according to the Leary doctrine. Vanessa dug into the rich mahogany bar as she contemplated the big man's fall from grace. She once loathed him, then loved him, now fears and pities him. Should she leave, could she leave? This was all she has known since that night and the glory and excitement of the job beat anything she saw on the outside world during her recruitment process every year. "It's gonna be what it's gonna be," she whispered to herself, one of her father's favorite sayings.

"Aaaaight let's get this show on the road!" The big man bellowed as he strutted nude past the bar area toward his studio apartment sized closet, breathing like he just ran a marathon. "Nothing wrong with a little drink before the dance," he added.

Vanessa stood shocked that he could sense she had taken a drink, but not too fearful, as the years of dedication and loyalty allowed her certain passes.

"We had an escape tonight, there was a civilian casualty," she stated in a monotone voice.

"It happens," the big man replied throwing his game night suit over his gigantic form.

"Never on game night it doesn't," with a worrying tone leaving her lips.

The Sixth emerged from the closet, "You worry too damn much. My population increase and bio testing have shown great strides. See, you and the men that came before me only saw them as amusement. I alone will unlock the great Goblin mystery and in the process, develop new human enhancement drugs that will make the current pharma advancements look like a school child's science fair failure."

Vanessa smiled and nodded in uncontested agreement. "They staying here?" She pointed to the two naked whores climbing onto the gigantic bed scrambling to find the remote for the wall sized television.

"Yeah, and have Rex and William bring me a male and female glamour after the conclusion tonight," Lionel replied as he made his way past the bar.

Vanessa swallowed a retort, his favorite for sure, but even she knew not to test him. They both left the suite and marched down the hall followed by the two armed staff members. The elevator dropped a few inches when the Sixth got in. Another fifty pounds and we are going to have to chopper his ass out of here, Vanessa thought as they made their decent.

4

Rex exited the expensive golf cart and strode toward the contestants like a perfect proud peacock. Hoping his strong demeanor would instill confidence into the lambs before the slaughter. He began his speech going over all the training they had received the days prior, marching frantically between them. A final desperate attempt to light a fire, but these flames held only a flicker of life and were about to be extinguished by a cold green wind. Year after year the contestants grew weaker, thinner, and more doped out. The allure of the games and the bounty it held were no longer enough to draw proper warriors. High end attorneys kept the hardened criminals living large on the inside and the homeless population were more interested in their next fix than the opportunity of a new lease of luxury living. This lot would be lucky to make it to their starting positions, Rex thought, as he finished his locker room speech.

Frail ducks in a row they all waddled their way to the weapons table. Swords, axes, crossbows and other instruments of death were laid perfectly across the massive wooden table. Several of them began to shake as they picked up the heavy weapons, effects from the adrenaline shots they were given an hour prior. Ten more carts pulled in on time up the path ready to load up the lambs.

"Six more hours, lads and fortune and glory await you!" Rex shouted as they shipped off into the dark devil's playground.

A few gave shouts, but their eyes spoke louder, those were eyes of deadlights heading into impending doom. Most were murderers, rapist, and drugged out vagabonds, but Rex's heart still sank a bit watching them disappear into the darkness. He spent the last three days with them and despite their evil past, the games had a way of cleansing their spirit. All the macho and bravado seemed to flee their souls during day one induction, leaving them stripped down to their basic primal beings. Most had not known fear or contemplated their mortality, the sight of the first Goblin had a way of invoking both instantaneously. Some would be spirited by the challenge, some would try to flee, but most began to accept their fate. This lot all choose the later. The sinking feeling of his heart was a good thing, having empathy meant after nine years of horror, he still had a soul.

Lionel and Vanessa had one last go around the basement control room. Air space, satellite coverage and cellular reception were all blocked over the ten mile perimeter of the grounds. A task that was becoming more expensive year after year and not just monetarily. The favors the Lionel empire provided to the puppeteers were bound to be discovered by the relentless media one day. Accompanied by their guards, both made their way to the elevator and ascended to the main floor. Lionel was downright jovial which made her uneasy. Was he so delusional now that he should think these games would go well?

She always spent the final day of training with the contestants recounting her glory to try and inspire the them. This year's group would not last an hour against a rabid pack of poodles yet alone blood thirsty Goblins. Loud chatter and applause greeted them as the elevator doors opened to the great grand hall. Vanessa, careful to stay two steps behind the man, struggled to stay composed as they marched through the parting crowd to the veranda. One of the smallest guests lists she had seen, but the usual suspects cheered loudly in anticipation of the one of a kind gladiator event. Columbian coke lords sung in Spanish, Japanese whales sprouted cheers from their blowholes and of course several of the American elite gave U.S.A. chants as they walked through the hall and into the crisp fall night. The one percenters followed them to the gigantic stone patio like buffalo with million dollar hides. Perfectly groomed staff handed them their game tablets, filled with grounds GPS, video coverage and gambling applications. Everything and every angle were made ready for the distinguished crowd. Armed security followed the crowd as they made their way off on to the multi-mile stone bridges which encompassed the playing field. Fat heads were glued to their devices, ready to pick out which sector would be best for viewing the slaughter or place their wages on man or beast. The wind carried screeches from the east causing Vanessa to shoot a glance to the farm and goosebumps erupted over her perfect pale skin. She steadied herself and raised the radio to her slightly quivering mouth, "Rex, the party is in place. We ready for the horn?"

"Ten-four," Rex replied, with the slightest sound of nervousness accompanying his response.

Fitzgerald, the head British butler appeared on que holding the old mountain horn. He handed the blower to the big man, careful to make sure the boss had a firm grip before letting his long slim fingers relinquish the ancient heirloom. Lionel held the small end to his thin lips and exhaled his entire being into the horn. A thunderous sea vessel sound rang thru the forest signaling the start of the slaughter.

Rex heard the signal accompanied by the three beeps on his radio. It was time to release the rage. He punched in the code on the security panel and the ten foot steal lock slowly rose unlocking the giant gate. Once the lock stood at midnight the titanium doors crept open. A green swarm fled from the farm, twenty in all to start, one for each contestant. Rex advised to go ten at a time this year at the pre-game dinner, but like most of his wise advice, it was ignored. Half the creatures sprinted right into the dark wooded arena, ignoring the weapons and deer meat laid out in front of the gates. Way too much adrenaline, Rex thought, the man took blood thirsty ancient creatures and put them on steroids. This was like giving a tiger a key bump. A few stopped and dined on the rancid meat, while the smarter of the bunch examined the rusty weapons lying on the fall floor.

"Rex, second herd is lined in position, let us know when to release," one of his guards radioed in.

"Hold steady, I'll keep you posted." Rex answered knowing damn well there would be no second wave of attack tonight.

The Sixth of his name parked his ass on the large cushioned bench and gazed up at the theatre sized screen sitting on the edge of the veranda. The screen was cut into the ten sectors of the playing field, with a rolling in game betting screen sliding down the side.

Most were playing heavy on the massive Mexican, who looked harder than a coffin nail. Vanessa knew they would collect big on that one, El hombre pissed himself when he toured the farm and the greenies feed on fear. The first encounter happened all too fast. Two smaller Goblins discovered the dope sick vagabond Vanessa found two months earlier in a rehab house in Baltimore. She was stunned to see the druggie's nerve hold as he fired a perfectly placed arrow through the eye of one of the creatures. Perhaps this crew would pull of an upset for the ages. The second Goblin got to him before he could reload and they tumbled to the leaf covered ground. Once on top of the man, the green freak tore chunks of meat from the man's defensive forearms. Two more greenies appeared, smelling the human blood and surged toward the smorgasbord. Hearing the big man laugh at the sight of the scene sent her tummy in a whirl. Had he now become even worse than the monsters, was any humanity or empathy left in him?

Laughter turned to eerie silence over the course of the next few minutes. As predicted, the Goblin hoard took out their weak opponents swiftly. Ten down in twenty minutes with only one green casualty to account for. The worst start to the games in history. Fitz brought the boss his Nicaraguan cigar and bottle of pure Absinthe and placed it neatly on the glass table in front of him,

Lionel made no attempt to enjoy either. Despite their training, two contestants climbed clumsily way up a giant maple, while several greenies chopped at the base.

"They were instructed not to climb, yes?" The boss asked, fury rising in his voice.

"Of course, but . . ." Vanessa started, but was quickly cut off by the rising of his pudgy hand.

Just one hour in and nineteen human corpses decorated the arena and nineteen Goblins remained. The giant Mexican fell fast as well, with a greenie placing a perfectly accurate blow with its ax to the tanned man's ankle, separating the foot and leaving hombre helpless. Almost too accurate for a mindless beast, Vanessa pondered. She took note that they were working almost as a pack now as well. When one would get into a spat, the creature would let out a new snarling sound, signaling the others. She stared blankly at the screen as the last helpless soul made way to the lagoon sector. The stocky man barely made it knee deep in the water before a green wave swept over him. Several of the creatures drug him underwater, emerging shortly after with chunks of flesh and bone hanging from their hideous sharp teeth. Sixty-five minutes in and the quickest Goblin Gauntlet in history was over. Only the shrieks carried by the October air broke the dead silence on the patio.

Lionel summoned Fitzy with a wave, "Have my room cleared. I'll be alone tonight."

"Yes sir," the stoic blank man replied.

The Sixth stood and turned to Vanessa with his face full of fury. "See everyone off. Proceed with the cleansing. I want everyone in the war room at eight p.m. tomorrow . . . everyone."

Vanessa nodded and immediately headed to the path entrance eagerly, not wanting to be anywhere near the big man. For the first time ever, she saw something in his glare, embarrassment. A reckoning would follow. Guests began to make their way back to the start of the path, disgusted and disappointed painted pallets decorated their fat faces.

"Loch, we all wrapped up?" Rex radioed in.

"Yeah, mop up," she quickly responded.

Two stars of film made their way quickly toward Vanessa looking to give her an ear full. A gigantic roar came from the farm area startling the stars. A new rash of bumps covered Vanessa's body again. She had never heard such an explosion of screams in unison. This was no mindless babble of beasts, this was a victory chant. This was no cry from creatures, this was evolution.

5

Four hours after the last man fell, Rex and his two best marksmen were still hunting the green devils from their stone perches. After the go ahead from Vanessa, Rex and William took out the first dozen quickly. Still feeding at the lagoon, they were green sitting ducks. The rapid fire cut through their nasty bodies like a warm knife thru soft butter, sending the remaining seven sprinting into the wooded darkness. A little after five a.m. and three remained as the first auburn light started to cut through the sky announcing the arrival of November. Rex removed his goggles and wiped his tired eyes. He began a slow march back to the main tower and let out a loud grunt. Several hours of crouching over stone was taking its toll on his fifty-five year old war torn body. The weary warrior stretched and gazed into the night, the fact that no one from the main house had checked in only intensified his growing anxiety. These games had never ended so quickly and the cleansing had never taken so long.

"I've got a visual," William radioed in.

"Where we looking, Will?" Rex asked.

"Courtyard, all three. They still look wired," William replied back.

"Hold, I'll be there in five. Declan, meet me there," Rex instructed his lads.

"Ten-four," Declan, the youngest and best shot in the squad, confirmed.

It had to be the damn courtyard, Rex thought, as he quickly walked to that sector. A quarter mile of stone rubble, giant columns and marble arches adorned that part of the park. The Sixth had constructed it a few years back to break up the monotony of the forest arena. It worked too, some of the best battles had taken place in the mock decorated fallen stone village. Plenty of places to hide, climb and rest if need be. Great for the games, bad for hunting prey. The thought of a ground sweep with the team gave Rex the chills, but if they could not wrap it up soon that was the only option. William was already in place when the boss arrived. His free hand held up in a clenched fist signaling silence. Rex crept to the edge of the wall and glanced toward the maze of white rubble looking for anything green. He saw one of the bastards darting beneath a small bridge thirty meters away. William saw it first as herd by the cracking of his Austrian Steyr, the world class rifle exploded in a short spurt. Seconds later the left side of the Goblin's head exploded in a red mist. An instant later Rex herd a growing whizzing sound pass over his bald head, then another come from left to right. His eyes followed the second sound and they rested on the sight of a steel arrow embedded in his star pupil's temple. William's head tilted at an unnatural angle, a river of blood droplets pouring from his wound. Rex's military instincts kicked in and he immediately fired wildly towards the flight from were the death blade came from. His SR 25 ripped stone, marble, and bark, hitting the giant trees beyond the stone. The wildfire hit the assassin and the monster plunged from his high position to his death, ripped nearly in two by the barrage of bullets. Blood drunk, Rex focused on the lifeless creature's corpse and unloaded another clip turning the thing into green goo. He would not have stopped if not for Declan's shout. Rex turned to see Declan holding his friend up, eyes watered and his face sheep white.

"Sir, call the doc!" Declan pleaded.

"He's gone son. Stay here, head down, don't move till I've told ya." Rex commanded and took off to take down the final star of the show. Fueled by rage and vengeance, he sprinted toward the main tower.

The mad Aussie threw his rifle on the weapons table and grabbed a simpler glock then threw open the hand to hand arsenal door and pulled a katana sword from its frame. Two of his crew just stood at attention, frightened to utter a word.

"Last location?" he questioned with steel reserve to the two shaken souls.

"It's in sector one headed toward the farm entrance," the older of the two replied.

Rex nodded and made his way to the metal ladder, descending with pace but caution with the sharp blade cuddled in his large left hand. At the base of the tower, Rex broke several compound laws all at once with no hesitation and took off into the early November morning. Taking all of five minutes, the highly trained soldier picked up the beast scent and tracks. It appeared to be circling the entrance to the farm then heading back toward the main house gates. His initial rage subsided and Rex was able to hunt with complete focus. A liquid sound broke the eerie silence, the fucker was near by and having a piss. Thirty yards away the Goblin was leaning against a giant oak, relieving itself of the night's drink. Rex jogged slowly towards his target, raising the sword for a death blow, but his heavy boots signaled the impending attack. Glancing over its hunched shoulder the Goblin spotted the madman approaching with pace and took off to the right. The primal beast, fearing the assault ran right into a dead end by the entrance of the main house instead of into the open forest. Rex closed in on his target quickly and was in striking distance when the Goblin shimmed backwards and attempted to take off in the opposite direction. Its fleet feet almost made it past Rex, but the trained man got a hold of the creatures tail just in time and with a swift harsh blow severed the appendage. A monstrous shriek nearly busted Rex's eardrum as the green demon fell to the frosted floor. Unholstering his glock, he unloaded on the thing until the clip was dry. Panting like a starved dog, Rex finally took a deep breath for the first time since he saw his pupil fall. He prepared for a bad night; he got a disastrous one.

6

Vanessa entered the solemn dark board room and quickly made her way past the brass of the games. All of them hiding their concerned faces by planting them firmly to their electronic devices. A few glanced up to give Loch a nod, which she reluctantly returned. At least eight of the ten top tier were responsible for the epic cluster fuck of the previous night, encouraging every sick request the big man proposed. Mindless blood thirsty green Goblins were not enough. They just had to be made stronger, faster, and now they appeared to be working together. The future never bodes well for those who mingle with the devil's toys, she thought, plotting herself down in the luxurious leather chair.

Everyone was ten minutes early, with one notable exception, Rex. His chair, adjacent to her seat and encompassing the big man's throne, sat empty. Rex was always the first one at all meetings and his absence made her heart flutter. William's fall exacerbated the debacle of the previous night. Whispers of Rex's revenge spread through the castle like an army of spiders' freshly spun webs covering the great rooms and dormitories alike. Vanessa swallowed her tears as one of the chefs broke the news to her at lunch. She slept right through breakfast. The security team were the only members of this fucked up family she could stomach. Simple soldiers performing simple duties, and hand selected by the honorable Aussie. On occasion she took a few of them to bed with her when urges overcame discipline.

A blind eye was turned on carnal rules. Seventy people, willingly confined to a specific area for years on end, were going to hump on occasion. The Sixth threw weekend parties once a month for the staff to indulge their every need, but that was not enough. Vanessa never enjoyed William. He was a stone-cold soldier like his boss and took to the rules as commandments. His passing did hit the cold women harder than she imagined. What of the Aussie though? Surely, he wasn't sent home or worse. Only six times in all of her years had an employee been terminated. Rightfully so on all occasions for breaking their sacred omerta. Induction phase for new employees and the code of conduct should be enough to keep even a media dog muzzled, but the temptation of revealing the games was too much for a few to resist. How could they not know that he would know? He knows everything, everyone, and at all times.

Two familiar loud voices echoed through the hall and into the room, one with an accent. Vanessa cracked a relieved smile and let out an exhale as Rex and Lionel appeared at the open door. Lionel looked surprisingly jovial and his commander, even more shockingly, appeared relaxed and refreshed. They circled the table like two apex sharks and strode towards their rightful seats at the head. Rex sat and shot Vanessa a reassuring smile, the Sixth stood over his enormous leather throne. Loud silence ripped through the room as the big man stared out into blank obedient faces. He gripped the expensive fabric with force and began.

"Shit happens."

Shit happens, that is the sum total of words this man has, Vanessa thought.

He continued with a smile, "Most of you in this room would eat a bag of Goblin shit with a smile if I asked you and with the salary you collect, you should. Others I know have thought me to go mad and perhaps I have, a bit. It is time to do what every great American businessman has done since the rising sun surrendered; I'm selling to the Japs." A collective curious groan broke out through the room.

"That's right, the time has come and the price is right. They got a nice secluded island in the Pacific and are ready to pay more money than the almighty himself. I would like to thank the docs for all of your advancements, the biological patents from your research alone will keep the Leary empire thriving for centuries. As for the rest of you, last night was not a failure but a resounding success. The greenies are more aggressive and intellectually advanced than ever before. We will continue with research up to three months before the final gauntlet. After the sale, those whose contracts are up are of course welcomed to enjoy your pretty pensions and leave us. Those still under the dotted line and those who wish to stay, I have a new set of games lined up while we bring the Seventh into the fold. For now, hold all questions and resume your daily duties please. Loch please stay with Rex and I."

Stiff shocked bodies slowly rose and cautiously exited the sterile board room. Vanessa leaned back in her chair, a thousand thoughts thundering through her temple. What biological patents? What new games? How the hell were they going to transport a hundred unknown mythical creatures without being seen?

Lionel flung his massive frame down in the chair and spun towards her, "Questions, my dear?"

Not even knowing where to start, she began simply, "Um, so what is needed of me?"

"Well darling, I put a silk head on a pig with that speech. Last night was a fuck up of biblical proportions. The Asians have been pestering me to sell for a decade but last night I had a revelation. No one gives a shit anymore about degenerates dying, no matter how dramatic the fashion. I now know why they stopped public crucifixions, obviously people got bored with them. For the final dark Goblin night, we are gonna need some people that matter and that is your one and only task this year. We will assemble five contestants that at one point or another were known in this world. The other fifteen will be comprised of our usual stock of prison filth, but I'm giving you an open purse to pull the meanest son of a bitches you can find."

"And the future of the games?" she questioned, trying to process the influx of information that just rattled her entire world.

"Well ya see, I do realize these green fuckers are wild ass animals and eventually one of the greenies is gonna get out for good. Honey, we are going A.I., that's right, automated robotic monsters for the next century for the family. Shit one goes looney and we just pull the plug." Lionel had not seen the Terminator films, she thought.

The big man rose as he started his exit, "I know what I have become and I see the way you both look at me. Rex is done after this year and Loch you may enjoy your freedom as well, in fact I'm pretty sure the Seventh is gonna want his own team to take over once he comes into his own. Little bastard is even more ambitious than I ever was. I don't say it often or ever, but all of your work is appreciated more than you will ever know. Let's make this the grandest gauntlet ever."

II
SET

7

Two days after the Christmas day killings, Rex was staring at the conductor of the symphony of slaughter. Donnie "The Dagger" DeStefano took out five Albanian bosses at the Kimmel Center in Philadelphia. Straight out of a Puzo novel, The Dagger carved his family's revenge on the Eastern Europeans. How he pulled that off and escaped unnoticed during the night of the noel performance was something Rex was determined to discover. The Leary empire had long ties with the old families. In the seventies and eighties, the compound was allegedly used as a scare tactic to gather information and as a dumping ground for gel haired rats. These myths and rumors floated through the grounds like chatty spirits.

Besides the task at hand, there was little else to do during the long days between the gauntlet. Telling stories, fact or fiction, was a good way to pass the time in the den of devils. Rex believed these tales though he had seen what a starving Goblin could do to flesh and bone. Mostly tied in the rising empire of legitimate gambling, the Aussie had not seen any of the bosses at the compound for years. After finding William's replacement from his mercs-r-us catalogue, Rex was shocked and perturbed when the big man turned down his appointment.

"Sorry mate, I've filled the position," Lionel explained on Christmas eve, obviously aware of the upcoming Albanian assassination. Another bad omen, another commandment broken, Rex pondered anxiously. His selections had never been questioned before and all the traitors during his spell had come from the medical team or the house staff. Twenty-eight years or older, at least two years military service and no immediate family. These were the minimum qualifications for application into the Goblin guard. With the exception of no children, Donnie did not possess the other two guidelines. Too hot to move, The Dagger was sent here to lay low for the year until his well-deserved Sardinian seclusion. Leary's loyalty and protection would be heavily rewarded. Mass breeding, the biggest export of goods the world had ever seen and now Rex had to keep an eye on the golden goombah.

Light exploded, taking over total darkness, in the media room as the induction video ended. Usually reserved after a final physical and psychological evaluation, Lionel wanted to put Donnie straight to work. Smart plan as well, keeping the brazen hitman occupied was the best way to keep him docile. After the wonder of the creatures wears off, boredom becomes dangerous. All the more dangerous for unproperly trained staff. Laughter and applause came from the front row of the epic theatre. The Dagger enjoyed the history of the gauntlet as if it were a midnight monster movie production. Rex strolled slowly from the back, leaving his drill instructor speech and demeanor behind. Years of psychological warfare training taught him to approach the young psychopath with ease.

"Now, that was fucking insane!" Donnie shouted.

"Enjoyed it did ya?" Rex asked.

"Fuck yeah. When do I get to see them?" Rex asked, pointing to the neon green exit sign smirking.

They both walked through the exit and into the mild West Virginian winter. Not much snow this year yet but the wind off of the Shenandoah cut through their exposed skin. Rex lead his trainee through a long narrow path, away from the main house and up to one of the entrances of the farm. Donnie's eagerness made him uneasy. No one should be this excited to see monsters. Did he not see the carnage and chaos these thing dish out? Was he just a born killer with no empathy or remorse? Several other frightening thoughts bounced thru the captain's bald head. A few minutes later they arrived at the entrance of the farm engulfed by a twenty-foot fence that encompassed the entire arena.

"This ok?" Donnie asked, pulling out a smoke.

"Yeah, can I bum one?" Rex answered, then taking his new employees offering and flicking it at the fence. The cancer stick sizzled on impact, fried to a quick crisp by the forceful electric current. Another fit of laughter flowed from Donnie's mouth, scaring Rex even more. Does nothing phase this fucker?

"Code 13, entering sector 1," Rex radioed in.

Electric humming filled the quiet air and then silence, followed by Rex punching in another code at the control box, sticking three feet from the fenced gate.

Making their way into the devil's playground, Rex said, "This will be your station," pointing to a plastic chair and the small shed that stood behind it.

The guardian at sector one was reserved for the weakest of his team. One would think the last barrier between the arena and the main house would be the most secure, but if the shit went down at this point, it was all she wrote. Lighting up anything green in this area was the only job for the sector one sergeant. Only three times in Rex's tenure had a greenie managed to get this close. He would keep Donnie busy, but when it mattered the young madmen would only have one menial job.

One mile later they approached the first of four sectors inside the farm. "Declan will be training ya over the next week for your guard responsibilities. But most of the damn time you will be working in teams herding and observing," Rex instructed.

"Sounds simple boss, so where da hell are they?" Donnie asked, looking up at the large modern barn about two hundred yards away from the entrance.

"Well, a smart guy like you studied that film pretty well. You should know they are viciously nocturnal. Like a green vampire the daylight seems to wear them down. Don't get too comfy during the day though, some play possum to get a go at fresh live meat. Once the night breaks they rise full of piss and vinegar. Ready to eat, fight and fuck. Two breeds of these beasts, blondies and reds. The blondies are shorter and more plump. They live up here," Rex explained, and then headed back up the wide trail to the house of the reds.

A few minutes later they both approached another fenced off section. "Reds are up in this one. Most rise to about five feet and are thinner but mean as coked up cobra. Up till about five years ago the blondies and reds use to have at each other on sight. Far as I can figure it was an ancient blood feud," Rex explained, trying to make some sense of this mad green world.

"But now they hardly scrap unless we are putting on a show or have a go at them ourselves, which we will be doing on occasion," Rex continued.

"They fucking talk?" Donnie questioned, more enthusiastic than ever.

"Nah, haven't heard anything even remotely close to words since I've been here. The big man has had teams of linguist through the years. Best bets are they communicate by tone, pitch and the signals they give with their tails. You see a tail shoot straight up tear that fucker apart quick. DNA shows them to be some what of feline in biology and the females give birth about every ten weeks, like a cat," Rex explained.

"Jesus, will you look at the cock on that thing!" Donnie shouted.

Rex nervously turned on a dime and gleamed toward the right of the perimeter. One of the reds was stumbling around in the mudded part of the little pond. This one was piss drunk and probably had no reason left in its already small wits. Not unusual but odd to see a greenie up and walking around mid-day. Rex brushed it off and started toward sector three of the living quarters, Donnie followed, still rambling about the size of the demon's dick.

"Yeah, we got them dressed up in cut off sweats most the time, but that one must have had a nice night out. We give them deer meat, water and stale beer. Seems to keep them happy. When the big man wants a show or if they act up we starve them and they start in on each other. Now, I'm thinking you're going to love this," Rex stated smiling.

No dull large barn sat up on the hill at this sector, but a gorgeous farmhouse. Donnie had to take out stock down south one time when a dixie boy tried to hold out on the family. The southern house looked like a shed compared to this country mansion. Rex walked right thru this perimeter, which was not guarded by any control box. The Dagger, a quick learner, paused before he followed his new boss.

"It's ok Donnie, we don't need to secure this area," Rex shouted a ways ahead now and impressing Donnie by sensing his hesitation with his back turned to him. They climbed the front of the wrap around porch and entered thru a thick black door. Attractive stained hardwood and plush furniture greeted the two at the hall entrance. Rex signaled to the seats by the stairs and they both took a brief rest.

"Well you had a quick glimpse at one of the beasts and a full film feature of the gruesome ghouls. Now this shit is going to shock ya. There are anomalies. Human, feline, ghouls sent from the devil himself. No one really knows what the hell these things are. We call them Goblins because that's what fiction and lore labeled them. Personally, I believed they were just some color tainted hillbilly mongoloids when I first took the gig. Then I saw one of these," Rex explained.

He then radioed in to Declan, instructing him to bring one down. Donnie's eyes followed Rex's to the top of the staircase, wide and wild with anticipation. Declan emerged shortly after with a chain leash wrapped around a greenie. No hideous large headed, small bodied, monster of myth was attached to the end of the link. A perfect female form followed her capture down the carpeted steps and into the open space of the grand hall. Still small, about four foot ten, and skin still green as a toad's ass, but the rest of her was a near perfect replication of any young star of the screen. Long curly blonde hair wrapped around her shoulders and covered her pointed ears. An angelic round face sat on top of her slender neck with two neon green eyes fixed in between a small sloping nose. Perfect breast hidden under her tight-fitting t-shirt, but too large not to protrude thru the cotton. Declan spun the Goblin princess around and her smooth green tail wagged thru the whole cut thru the small athletic shorts. Spun around once more for the onlookers and then the monster model was led back up the stairs.

"You got two hundred grand on you?" Rex asked.

"Not at the very moment," Donnie responded, still wearing his love goggles.

"Then don't even fucking think it!" Rex sprouted loudly to get the point across.

The Aussie stood and made his way back to the front door. Donnie still in a daze, slowly followed, thinking once his funds were released, he was definitely taking a spin on that thing.

Silence followed the two as Rex let his eager employee calm down as they entered the last domain of the housing fields. Several large stables circled about fifty yards of a small dirt clearing. Inside the circle, ten children Goblins kicked and threw plastic toy balls at each other. You could forget these were blood thirsty creatures watching the young ones play and laugh. Rex made sure that Donnie got a good look at them. Once The Dagger settled in watching them and broke his first smile, Rex sent a crackled message thru his radio.

"Three are limp, eliminate," he signaled.

Not a second later, three of the small one's heads burst and red mist sprouted over their playmates. Shrieks followed.

"Those three wouldn't make the cut," Rex spoke to a stunned Donnie. "We don't fuck about here son," he finished and walked back toward once they came.

The look on Donnie's face gave him satisfaction. He took no pleasure at all in killing the young ones regardless of how he knew they would turn out. But, he had to show this man something beautiful and horrible to gage if The Dagger had any human emotion left after years of being a hired killer. Shocked and solemn was the look on Donnie's face, which was a welcomed relief to the Aussie. There was humanity yet left in the ginney gunman after all.

8

Vanessa slipped on the frozen sidewalk as she made her way to the run down gym. Tommy grabbed her before she took a total tumble, hugging her slender body in his large bicep. Now steady, she resumed her power walk up to the entrance, welcomed by a red door with chipped paint. Tommy and Vincent entered first and the smell of sweat and despair filled their nostrils. A quick glance around and she was thankful for her large escorts. A dozen boxers seized their training and glared at the attractive women dressed in designer clothes. No words came from the athletes, but their eyes saw a five-star meal walk in and they were starving.

Having been through the toughest prisons in the country, Loch was not accustomed to feeling uneasy. For the first time since her night of glory she was afraid. Despite her armed escorts, if this crew wanted to take them, they could. Tommy headed over to one of the trainers and announced their arrival. Their recruitment trip had gone very well so far. With the expanded purse, Vanessa had secured ten top flight contestants but still not a one notable name and she needed five for the boss.

The trip to River Rouge, Detroit, was her third attempt to pull in a real name. Tommy signaled for his companions to head to the back. Sounds of dusty speedbags and rope hitting their marks returned as they walked through the training center. The stench got worse as they made their way to the old locker room in the back.

He was there, giving instructions to a small Hispanic boy. At least the young fighter looked small in the presence of the champ. Tyrone "The Terrible" Taylor held the greatest prize in the world for six months many years before. Undefeated up until his first defense of the crown and then the world swallowed him up and spit him out. After winning the title, Taylor went on a mad rampage. Several assault charges, a weapons confiscation and thirty pounds of weight gain, the champ got slaughtered on his first title defense. The spiral had only begun, once life and his entourage ate up his entire fortune he began to eat everything in sight. After two come back attempts and ballooning close to four hundred pounds the champ was done. Closer to three hundred pounds these days, his tired face looked older than its fifty-two years should. Those two giant anvils attached to his massive torso still looked like they could kill a man with one swing. Vanessa waited for the training sermon to conclude and the young man to exit before she began with a smile.

"Mr. Taylor, it is an honor to meet you. I believe our office had alerted you to our arrival," Loch started.

"Yes ma'am," the giant man responded and slowly took a seat on the worn wooden bench.

In response, Vanessa walked toward him and took a seat at the other bench adjacent to his. Apparently, this was the office, she thought to herself, trying not to grimace as the puddle of sweat soaked into her pants.

"The Leary Corporation would like to make you an offer, Mr. Taylor. If accepted and contract fulfilled, you would be eligible for a payment of three million dollars with taxes and fees taken care of by the Leary estate. We have researched your current economical situa . . ."

"I'll do it," the old warrior cut her off.

Vanessa sat stunned. She had spent over two hours with the last two big names on her fallen stars hit list. Once she went over the fine lines, both sent her packing. Both of them were down and out, but they weren't down and out and down for the count. Apparently, Mr. Taylor was.

Tyrone lowered his head and spoke softly, "I'm sure you know the bank is going to take this place soon and you are not sitting in a locker room, you are sitting in my bedroom. I got a few friends left in this miserable world, but I've never been and never will be a burden. So, whatever it is, and I'm sure it's bad, I'm at the last round ma'am and the final bell is about to ring."

"Mr. Taylor, I can assure you that I would not be here unless you have every chance of getting that money and starting over."

"Don't have to kill any kids or women, do I?"

"Not at all. Let me give you the broad strokes."

Warm leather seats heated Vanessa's frozen ass as the SUV pulled away from the gym. She should have been in a joyous mode and gleaming to break the news to the boss. The former heavyweight champion of the world was going to be in the gauntlet. Instead of making the immediate celebratory call, Loch stared thru the tinted windows at the icy ghetto surrounding the gym. Her heart broke a little recapping the champ's quick responses to her information session. Allegedly he was in decent health and knew he would have to pass a physical in September, assuring her he would go into training very soon. Lionel paid out to all contestants, usually a couple hundred grand to beneficiaries of the fallen. She thought him noble for that until she discovered the gambling receipts one year. One whale's loss covered ten years of victim pay outs and the house always wins.

When the champ signed the beneficiary papers over to the church her soul sank, not even a family member was fit for any fortune, obviously the man was all alone. Her fingers hit the control panel on the side of the door and the window slowly crept down. A blast of winter air felt good on her saddened face and her chalk white cheeks turned red instantly. Water filled her eyes from equal parts sadness and the freezing wind. Closing her eyes, Vanessa tried to envision him winning, resting in a nice home in a better environment, perhaps being able to love or be loved again. Almost by design the SUV dipped and swerved as it hit one of the hundreds of potholes welcoming them back into the city. Reality hit her with the thumping of the vehicle. Tyrone may be able to fight his way thru a few hours, but regardless of how hard he trained, how many greenies he could knock out, no way in hell would he last the full six. At least the church was going to get a major renovation.

9

Nearly two feet of snow was left after the blizzard had blown north. It was the worst storm Rex had seen since his tenure started. When the second storm hit the night before panic set in through the grounds, even the big man looked concerned from the frigid forecast. His men worked tirelessly through the three days and did a damn good job. All of the paths were cleared and not a one incident in the process. Greenies loved the night snow, but posed little threat as they found it hard to navigate too quickly in the white powder.

A well deserved reward was awaiting all the staff as announced at lunch. January's monthly wild weekend was cancelled due to extreme breeding sanctions. It had gone well and it looked like they would easily hit their delivery quota for the Asians come October. At first, Rex was concerned with the prospect of over population, but to his surprise the extra fortifications and procedures kept the greenies more docile than he had ever witnessed. No escape attempts and the in fighting between the monsters was at a minimum. An even more welcomed surprise was the performance of his newest team member. Expecting an egotistical maniac, Donnie proved his worth. Hard working, taking orders without question and performing with a positive attitude had shocked the Aussie. Perhaps the training of contract killers was closer to a military regiment than he considered. Too many mob movies clouded his judgement.

The men enjoyed Donnie as well, his tales of the wild life were welcomed entertainment to a bunch of grunts. Better than any films or books that filled the media center, the real-life tales told by the hotshot mob kid dwarfed any cinematic rendition. Rex had to admit the assassination of the Albanians was one hell of a yarn even if it may have been embellished a tad.

Things had gone well since the last gauntlet, too well perhaps. Change was swirling soon, faster than the West Virginian wind and Rex needed to focus. More important, his staff needed the monthly break bad. The worst part of a fine running operation was the impending letting down of their guard. Over the course of his time, routine and boredom led to an inevitable break down. Clearing his head, Rex hopped in the small cart and slowly made his way to the glamour house to check on the beauties before setting up the shifts for the weekend. Four would stand guard at a time while the others would enjoy food, drink and women. Perhaps he would take someone to bed this weekend, it had been far too long, but the penicillin shots that followed on occasion were a bitch to take.

Heavy flurries from the mounds of snow drifts blocked Rex's vision but he could see that none of the three guards were at the front door of the Victorian farmhouse. Not that any of his staff would risk the reprimand of screwing around with a glamour, but these three were veterans of the compound and their absence made him uneasy. On cue, the emergency horn sounded and exploded into the early evening air. Rex jumped from the cart and pulled his hand piece as he sprinted to the lavish home. He stopped at the front steps and ran back quickly to the cart to get the automatic from the undercarriage. Thirty rounds would not do if he had to shoot his way to safety. Experience took over and he calmly radioed into the staff for updates. Responding in proper order before he could make his way back to the house, everything was fine at the gates, but the silence from the three at the house sent a sweat streak running down his brow. The emergency horn at this location was in the back kitchen where the gorgeous Goblins got to gorge on cooked meat and fresh fruits. Two glamours, chained to post by the stairs, welcomed the Aussie with frightened eyes. They both pointed to the back of the home and he followed their direction by pacing slowly in that direction, careful to keep his pistol pointed at them before leaving the room. They may be model monsters, but monsters none the less and a few had taken a bite or two out of staff and guest over the years. Winter wind shot past Rex as he entered the kitchen cautiously, the large sliding doors were wide open. Once he headed out onto the stone porch spurts of gunfire deafened the howl of the noisy wind.

"Everyone hold at sector one, stay on alert," Rex instructed his crew, careful to keep a monotone voice to ease panic. Not wanting to start a stampede nor have his lads come rushing into a snowy ambush.

The sight of the three standing and shooting at the back of the glamour house yard gave him a quick moment of relief. His shouts were drowned out by gunfire and loud currents of winter air. Reaching the first of his men, Rex saw what had drawn them out into the yard and he quickly commanded a retreat. At least twenty reds were climbing the back perimeter fence, several had made it over and were storming toward the men. Another short spurt from the four and the greenies dropped into the shoveled shallow snow.

"House, now!" Rex shouted, as he stepped in front of them allowing them to sprint back to the house.

A glamour lay face down by the fence, her head held into the soft snow by a red who was entering her by force. Rex fired two quick shots, one for a kill, one for mercy, then turned and made his retreat. Once inside the kitchen, he sealed the doors shut and with the help of one of the grunts, pushed the large sitting table against the wall.

"Are all the fences up," he shouted into his radio. A few seconds of static felt like hours before a response.

"Boss, looks like they went down a few minutes ago, trying to reboot," Declan replied.

Millions in electronics in the basement of the main house and they can't electrify a fucking fence, he mumbled to himself.

"Back up now boss," an excited Declan radioed.

"Ten-four, send me five quickly for clean up," Rex demanded immediately.

After the reinforcement arrived, they went on a sweep of the yard. Another red was on top of the glamour's corpse when they got to the perimeter and another of Rex's bullets took it out. Besides that, the area was clear. With the electric back up he could wait till morning before a full sweep between the sectors. A few dozen branches rested outside the fence where the reds started their siege. This was disturbing to the captain, basic perimeter testing tactics. These damn creatures were getting too damn smart. After securing the glamour house, Rex questioned his men. All was well and then they herd a scream from the kitchen, the

Goblin girl had gone outside and was snatched up by a few reds. They cuffed the glamours downstairs to the post on the stairs and secured the upstairs before they began their rescue mission. By the time they got to the end of the yard the reds were pouring over the fence, Rex had showed up shortly after.

"Rex, the big man wants a report," Declan called.

"Be up shortly," Rex responded.

Driving slowly back to the main gate, the night's events replayed through his pounding head. It wasn't until he entered the back garage and saw the disappointed looks on his men's faces that he remembered. Yup, no party this weekend as there would be at least a two to three day search and clean up. They needed the break badly as well, perhaps he could talk the big man into a week long retreat for the lads. That request looked doomed when he saw The Sixth's furious expression as soon as he walked into media center.

10

Sweat broke out over Vanessa's body, dampening her expensive blouse. High in the eighties in early March, but the humid Florida air made it fell much more like ninety. Her bone white skin instantly turned a shade of blistering red as she entered the trailer park. At least a good mile walk down to the lake where allegedly her next acquisition was having a late morning swim. Where else would Sara The Sarasota Shark Sanders be? Rusted bikes, cracked lawn furniture and cheap empty beer cans decorated the lawns parallel to the cracked concreate path. Stained siding and ripped screens dressed the cruddy mobile homes as Vanessa strolled quickly past them. Several minutes later a cooling breeze from the lake welcomed her to the shoreline. Both the guards stayed back at the vehicle. One thing Loch knew was white trash, being a poverty princess herself in another life. This breed would be spying on her thru dirty windows and tear apart an unattended expensive SUV quicker than a NASCAR pit crew. Burnt grass replaced steamy concreate at the edge of the lake along with a very large, DON'T FEED THE GATORS, sign. Loch gave the tall grass surrounding her a quick but observing glance, avoiding being eaten by green things was her specialty after all. Fifty yards out two tanned arms propellered a wet mop of blond bobbing hair toward the shore. Salty sweat fell from Vanessa's lip into her parched tongue as she cracked a smile at the sight of her prey. The former Olympian still had it, darting toward the shallows like a swift serpent. Sara went under the surface for a second then stood breathing heavily thirty yards away from her stalker.

The Shark took her last steps from the water onto dry scorched land. Matted wet hair slunk down Sara's too thin body, glued to her bony ass which was covered by a confederate bikini of course. Cracked sun-soaked skin made The Shark look way older than her thirty years of age. Slow steps turned into a slow jog as she peered at Vanessa and made pace toward a rundown hot pink painted shack just up the hill from the lake.

"Ms. Sanders," Vanessa shouted, "I'm a fan and I have an amazing opportunity for you," now jogging as well and reverting to her native uneducated tongue.

"You wit intervention?" Sara yelped back as she reached her wooded porch.

"No, fuck, give me a second would ya," Vanessa panted, almost drenched from the fifty-yard dash.

Sara turned around giving the well dressed woman a once over before flinging open the torn screen door, shooting out a waving hand, welcoming Vanessa in. Green turf covered the small living room of the one-bedroom shack, shack being a favorable description. Sara signaled Vanessa to take a seat wherever, the torn sectional being the only option. Cheap domestic beer cans covered the table in front of the sectional followed by a small flat screen that shot back Vanessa's reflection as well as the giant frame that hung behind her. It was there, pressed in a plastic framed tomb, an Olympic Bronze medal.

Sara was a sensation heading into the games. A golden girl from the sunshine state, favored to swim her way to a sweep. The federation kept her dark side at bay and publicist presented the perfect poster girl. Coming in third in the first event sent her trailer park temper raging. Allegations of punching her coach, drinking before day two and sleeping with her teammate came out after the incident. In front of millions on day two, Sara had her leg clipped heading into the final lap of the relay. Simply splashing her opponent at the finish line would have gotten The Shark a small suspension but this shark had furious fangs. After head butting the Kiwi at the finish line, spilling bright red blood into the perfect blue pool, Sara choked and nearly drowned the Wellington Whale. Three teammates barley tore The Shark off of her opponent, but not before the New Zealander suffered minor brain damage and a permanent crook in her nose. From a celebrated shark to pariah piranha in one day, that was the beginning of the end for Sara.

Eight years on she frantically walked out of her back bedroom in an oversized t-shirt and cut off denim shorts, looking every bit Ms. Redneck 2020. Sara pulled two canned beers from a small fridge and sat next to Vanessa, offering her a drink. Loch took the cold can and quickly sipped out of respect for her host. Spoiled with imports and fine wine, her pallet nearly spit the pale ale out at first taste.

"What's the deal hun?" Sara questioned quickly, her tanned bare feet tapping the turf anxiously.

Vanessa started her pitch, "Ms. Sanders, I represent the Leary estate and we would very much like to invite you to a contest. The winner of which would receive a prize of five million dollars."

Loch started the bid a bit higher feeling empathy for the former aquatic angel turned demon of the depths. If not for Lionel, Vanessa knew she would be in a place perhaps not as nice as this, surrounded by a dead forest instead of a sorrowful swamp.

"Five mil huh? Who da fuck I gotta kill for dat?" The Shark questioned coldly. No stranger to exploitation offers, Sara had been on a few reality shows and one really bad late-night cable film, all of which ended badly. None of which had a price tag near this.

"Sara, I'm not going to tell you that the contest is not dangerous. What I will say is that I would not be here unless we felt you had a very good chance of winning. As well, simple participation entitles you to three hundred thousand, just for showing up and giving it a go," Vanessa offered, keeping it as vague as possible.

Sipping her beer and staring threw the screen door out to the placid lake, Sara seemed to drift away.

"You ok hun?" Vanessa interrupted the silence after what seemed an age.

"All of them took a piece of me. My family, my coaches, and my lovers. There's nothing left. Whatever this is, I'm down," Sara quietly accepting the offer, her eyes glossing over with water.

"I believe in you," Vanessa whispered, putting her hand on The Shark's muscular thigh. Sara gave Vanessa a lover's look, taking the reassuring hand as a pass. Seconds later their lager flavored lips locked.

Tommy and Vincent looked concerned as their boss marched toward them. Her blouse slightly torn and the little make up she had on scribbled around her mouth and eyes. Vanessa had taken women to bed before, but this was different. A sex starved shark had roughed her up a bit and her appearance showed it, but the rowdy romp was a welcomed surprise for Loch.

"Everything ok boss?" Tommy questioned as he opened the back door of the SUV.

"Two down, three more to go big boy," Vanessa smirked slightly.

11

Everyone at the compound looked immaculate for the inspection. Fitz personally inspected everyone and everything. Lime Clorox filled Rex's nostrils as he entered the main hall in anticipation of the Japanese entourage. Boss man literally cracked the whip after the bungle in the blizzard. Three of the staff were stripped, whipped and threatened to be a Goblin meal for the infractions that led to the rampage of the reds. Fear was the ultimate motivator; the entire operation never ran better since the reckoning that followed. Lionel himself even shaped up, acting more like a Goblin general than a mindless monster, even losing a good fifty pounds. Lionel left nothing else to chance while sending resounding reminders of how important the big sale was, buzzing in all of the staff's ears like an annoying bee. Heavy boots rumbled over the expensive marble floors announcing the arrival of his team. Tight neon green berets fastened to their heads and fitting black on black tactical uniforms covered their bodies. Rex hid a proud smile; he had built one nasty killing machine.

Fitzy entered and waved a long cold finger at the team, signaling them to the roof. Thunderous whirling sounds greeted the team on the top of the main building as the large helicopter settled onto the secured pad above them. Two large uniformed Asian men stepped out first, followed by three impeccably dressed Japanese kings. Their glorious grey suites only outmatched by their perfect full white hair. After bowing to the guest, Rex led the honored buyers to the dining hall where The Sixth awaited them.

Consistent laughter erupted thru out the power lunch as Rex stood outside the lavish door with only his two Asian counterparts as company. Two hours and none of the three so much as whispered a word, three silent sentinels. Closing his eyes for a only a moment, Rex envisioned the day these people would leave with the green horde and his watch would end. A tall Fosters at a shady pub on the sea was a welcomed image, helping to break the tense silent stand off with his guest. Another thought broke up his happy meditation. How they were going to get one hundred fifty plus greenies out of here was an unwelcomed question that was supposed to be answered today. A loud unlatching of the massive doors broke up his brief mental retreat and the inspection began. Rex followed protocol, as he always did, and waited for Lionel to take the lead. Following his boss as The Sixth led the group thru the media room exit and into the fresh April air.

All four sectors were combed over without a hitch. One hundred and seventy-two greenies and nine glamors were accounted for via visual and monitoring systems. Filled with sleeping agents the night before, most were passed out on the dirt lawns, weary from drugged food and the mid-day sun. Joyously satisfied by the look of it, the future owners of the Goblins followed Lionel excitedly toward the bio lab past the gates of sector four. Rex had not been in the bio center for a few months, right after the last batch of baby greenies were taken in. New chemical experiments were being conducted on growth was the email he got in March and that his clearance for that area was revoked until further notice. Any security issues near that building needed to be cleared with the man himself. Odd but not unusual, besides, he had seen some nasty chemical injures to the white coats in his time. Rumors were far less frequent thru the grounds since the bad February night, but it was said they were making a pill that would make Viagra look like a flintstone vitamin. This rumor was enough to keep the men well away from the lab area, no one wanted to be around if there was a leak, turning their junk into a gooey green Goblin cock. Hoots and applause rang in front of Rex as the pack had entered the observation room at the lab before him. Instinct kicked in when he saw what they were thrilled about and he went for his glock before reason settled in quickly. Twenty feet in front of him were three large titanium cages inhabited by nine-foot Goblins. Wonder and horror were splattered over his team's faces as they entered slowly behind him.

"Gooooozilla!" one of the purchasers shouted with glee, followed by laughter from his partners.

Hit the two Asian henchmen first, then Lionel, then the giant greenies, Rex's mind flashed at hyper speed. Confident it could be done quickly and equally confident his lads would back him. His appearance and movement gave away his plan as one of the Japanese guards stepped toward him, reaching toward his armed belt. Rex adjusted his stance and put on a more accepting expression. After the silent showdown, Lionel led everyone back to the roof to see off his buyers.

"Meet me in the war room!" The Sixth yelped, barely audible over the humming of the blades.

Rex nodded as he watched the big black bird take flight into the spring sky. Digging ferociously into his bald head, Rex could not get the image out of the giant green Goblins. Always confident he could take out four or five greenies hand to hand; he was sure that there would be no victory in any scrap with one of those massive devils.

"Relax for fuck sake," Lionel said, as he strode into the room with three large scrolls tucked under his right arm.

"What in the bloody fuck were those things?" Rex questioned, not really interested in the boss, employee, status que at this point.

"The Japs wanted to see how big they could breed them, gonna have them rampaging through the jungle terrain I'm told. Amazing, aren't they?" Lionel answered very excited.

"Unstoppable, more like it. They could bite a man in two!" Rex exclaimed, nearly shouting now to exemplify the severity of the beast.

"You worry too damn much, suppose that's a good thing. Look we are only releasing one at the finale and two tranq darts still will knock them out. Enough of that for now, I got the transport plans," Lionel finished, laying down three big maps and explaining how they were going to get the greenies out for good.

After the meeting Rex walked out on to the massive veranda and lite up a cigar, usually reserved for his end of day reflection, but he needed to have a long quite think. Lionel and his partners were going to literally ship out what would be left of anything green the morning after the gauntlet. Rex's team would dart the little shits in schools of ten after the victory ceremony and cuff and transport them to several small boats in the Potomac about a mile down from the fourth sector. Once loaded all teams were going to take a nice slow sail down the Potomac, through the Chesapeake, and into the Atlantic. Two large Japanese ships would take possession of the cargo ten miles east of the Maryland shore. Lionel rambled on how they were going to go south past Argentina and end up north of New Zealand at some large jungled island that would be a new horror land. Reasonably, Rex thought it was a safe, solid plan and the big man had enough connections to block out their path for a good hour or so. Nearly gagging on his stogie, Rex cracked himself up thinking that one of the world's best kept secret was going to be cruising right past the Lincoln memorial.

12

Chopping up your wife and her secret lover to pieces probably would've gotten the smiling man sitting next to Vanessa ten years on good behavior. Slicing up the two responding officers got you the needle in the great state of Texas. Heavy was the price for the swordsmen's early parole to the compound and the new identity he would assume should he last the night, but Vanessa was confident this one would be worth every penny. Planning such escapes frighten Vanessa in the past, until she saw what real money could buy. His death would be faked on the inside, no one would have a close look at a cop killer's unfortunate demise and the warden would get a hefty new pension package. Once the man was escorted out of the room Vanessa dropped her serious corporate demeanor and cracked a smile. Good news, she had filled her supporting roles cast. Bad news, she still needed three stars for the show to go on. It was early May and her list was growing thinner by the day. Inquiring texts started coming from the boss, digital clouds before the storm. Now five months on the road, her and the two men were growing weary. She stared past the open door wondering if she was going to be able to pull this off when Satan himself sent her a demon of sorts. Unless her tired eyes failed her, Mike The Mountain Mouldon just walked past the door in full guard gear. Loch picked up the phone mounted to the table and rang the warden. Several minutes later the fat warden, smelling of cheap whiskey, obviously celebrating his new fortune to come, confirmed it was indeed The Mountain. A newly wealthy warden went to fetch the big dog eagerly upon Vanessa's request. Grabbing her tablet, Loch quickly refreshed herself on the exploits of her new prospect.

Six foot seven and fast as a West Texas coyote, the famous longhorn had pro teams tanking games just for the chance to get him in the first round of the draft. Collegiate rumors were overshadowed by his glory on the gridiron. Mike was not just a great player; he was athletic evolution. As best they tried, once his last bowl game was done, not even the dark lord could keep a muzzle on the big dog at the combine. Yelling, "Hail Satan," every time he smashed a record at the combine was just the beginning. Videos of blood rituals, satanic seminars and eventually animal sacrifices started going viral. Obviously stolen by the holier than now league to exile the young man. Can't sell soft drinks or theme park vacations with the star of the show making pentagram signs at mid field.

Mike was raised by a satanic cult in the wasteland of the lone star state and from everything she was reading, he had the true faith, so much for freedom of religion.

Feeling more like an ant speaking to an elephant, Vanessa started, "How do you like your job, Mike?"

"Just fine ma'am," he briefly responded.

Such manners for a Satanist she thought. "I'm sorry that you were discriminated against, but I think I can shed some light upon your eternal darkness," Vanessa continued, impressing herself with the selection of words.

"Lucifer shines light into my heart everyday and allows me this great gift to guard his children from the demons locked in here," The Mountain preached.

"Would the dark lord be pleased with a five million dollar offering?" Vanessa pressed hoping the figure would break The Mountain's satanic stare. It did not as he continued with another dark sermon.

"Money is a snare used by Jesus to trap false worshippers. One can't put value on the eternal love Satan bestows upon us every day," Mike proclaimed, more serious than ever.

Spending fifteen years with real devils, Vanessa tested her resolve with one more offering. "How about seven million? I promise on everything unholy that I can introduce you to some of Lucifer's little green cousins."

The Mountain's eyes widened with wonder and curiosity as Vanessa leaned back on the uncomfortable metal chair grinning. That look from hell boy was all she needed to confirm she had a third star to throw at the West Virginian sky.

13

"Rex, you better get down to red town quick!" Declan yelped on the radio.

"What?" the annoyed Aussie replied, overseeing the wild west grounds that the boss just had to set up. A homage to the First and his exploits out west once the compound was up and running. Myth had it that with Goblins in toe, the first of his name, shook down some of the toughest crews in the American wild west. Going town to town collecting a hefty bounty for rounding up the monsters which his brother had hidden just outside the towns to harass the locals.

"Looks like I got a few dozen reds passed out all over the lawn, except they aren't moving, and I mean like not at all," the young sharpshooter reported.

"On my way," Rex responded, signaling a few of his lads to follow, they made their way past a fake salon and headed to the house of the reds.

Declan was right, about thirty reds were sprawled out over the short grass, now green from the early heat of May. Not uncommon for morning, but it was already late in the afternoon and the little bastards should be up and running around. Rex walked to within a whisker of the electric fence, they were not just passed out, they were dead asleep, no, they were dead. None of their chests or tummies rose and fell the slightest bit. A brief bolt of fear shot thru Rex as he closed his eyes and hoped it could not be. Five years ago, some bad meat got into the greenies and they lost about half the stock. Lionel flipped his shit that week and since then the venison went through a much tougher examination before being chucked at the Goblins.

"Turn red sector cold," Rex radioed to control and gave the signal for Declan and the other two to arm themselves. A soft buzz broke the silence, signaling the crew that it was safe to enter. Rex still slapped his boot against the fence before unlocking the front of the gate to avoid a nasty shock.

Twenty yards in and Rex leaned over the first red. One ugly fucker, yellow eyes stared the soldier down, long filthy red hair spread over the top of its head and was matted into the grass, its mouth was frozen in position exposing grey and light black pointed teeth. Rex leaned in toward the chest for a closer look, then pulling back, as he was hit with a whiff of the stench from the green skin. Security spent the most time with the greenies, but only on occasion would they get with in ten yards of any of them over child's age, forgetting how awful they stunk. Docile and beautiful glamours were different, feed proper food and bathed daily. Putting his boot on the red's chest checking for any signs before checking for a pulse, Rex feared the worst. No reaction from the creature signaled they were in for a shitstorm. Declan's count was correct, about thirty lay on the open field. How many more inside and what of the blondes? Even if they started mass breeding tonight, the bio boys could maybe only get twenty or fifty fully grown by the start of the gauntlet. Signaling with his raised hand, Rex instructed the others to have a look at the next three closest creatures. Walking slowly the lads spread out to complete their own experiments. After conducting their own exams, each one of the team gave Rex a slow side to side head shake. The big bald man was about to call for a fall back when searing pain ripped into the meaty part of his calf. Highly trained instinct kicked in and he fired three rounds into the little devil's head before comprehension set in. Shrieks shattered the spring sky and the green red-haired corpses rose quickly from their sham slumber.

"Fallll bacckk!" Rex shouted, as he quickly assessed the ambush.

Only twenty yards away from the gate, he and the other two would make it easy. But Declan had to go up the hill a way for his examination. Popping a few charging reds with ease, two of his team got past the boss and were at the gate quickly. Rex started towards his star shooter when an avalanche of green came bursting thru the barn. Declan had been jumped by two of the bastards while he took out his seemingly dead patient. Two shots from the Aussie freed Declan.

"C'mon son, move yer ass!" Rex commanded, as the green horde would be on top of them both shortly. Declan turned in response, his torn throat exposed. He gave Rex a wink and tumbled to his grassy grave. Shouts from the other lads broke up the horror show, snapping the sargent into gear. A few shots rang past him as he sprinted toward the gate. The more rapid the shots the closer they were to him until he passed the entrance and herd the snapping of the metal lock. Seconds later sparks flew as a dozen reds were stung hitting the fence with full force. Control room was thankfully watching and hit the juice once Rex was thru the gate. More shrieks of what could only be described as laughter shot out of the horde's green grotesque mouths. After catching his breath, Rex turned back to survey the surprise slaughter. Several of the reds were feasting on Declan. No revenge this time, no blood lust rampage, just acceptance crept thru his entire spirit. Like a good soldier, he radioed for clean up and went back toward the main house to give a report.

"Big Joey is sending us another one," Lionel explained to a quiet Rex.

"Sure, sounds good." Rex quietly responded.

Lionel continued, "You were worried about Donnie and look how good that turned out. These guys take orders well and we just have a few more months to go. We go full lock down here till the fall, I promise. We all need you sharp Rex. I can't pull this off without ya. Declan, William, we all know the risk."

"Ate him like a bucket of wings," Rex spoke to the open air, then started again. "When I started, these things fought, ate, drank and fucked until they passed out. Now they have a signal system, rarely have at each other and have the mind to set up a plan. Enhancement and advancement are not my specialty. I hunt and kill. Your white coats should take a bow. They took mindless beasts and turned them into intelligent killing machines. If you really are thinking clear Lionel, ship these things out now," Rex suggested.

"One hundred seventy-five days until it's all a memory," Lionel said, putting his pudgy hand on the sullen soldier's shoulder.

The Sixth turned and walked slowly away to his penthouse retreat. A memory Rex thought. Memories are for civilians; soldiers carry ghost and ghost haunt for a lifetime. Declan's ghost along with William's and his other fallen brothers would spook Rex until his last days.

14

Applause, like thunder, shattered through the Vegas theatre. Radu had just ascended through four giant propellers to the roof of the arena. He then flew over the crowd for his finale, ending up at the plank stationed at the back exit of the adjacent upper deck. Two large assistants met him at the roof top exit and untangled the invisible wire that gave the mystic an illusion of flight. Radu quickly made his way down the dressing room eager to get back to his wife and newborns. Randy, the head of security was waiting in the hall leading to the back.

"Mr. Rick, there's somebody waiting for you!" Randy proclaimed.

"What? Sunday shows are no meetings. Is it that dipshit from the magic union? Damn freaks want a fucking hand out every time we branch out," referring to the new illusionist phone application, giving the public tricks to the trade. A big no no in the world of hats and rabbits.

"I think not, sir. It's some woman and she must have clout because Mr. DeAngelo and his staff escorted her to your room," Randy stated, trying to keep up with the quick pace of the magic man.

Radu shot Randy a worried look. Going on year five at the palace and never had Mr. DeAngelo been to a show yet alone backstage. His pace quickened even more, eager to find out who this special woman was.

"Hello, Mr. Radu. Vanessa Vorner. I represent the Leary Corporation," Vanessa said, as the frantic looking mystic entered the room aggressively.

Radu gave a glance around and found no brass from the hotel there, just the attractive women standing with her hand outstretched. Radu accepted her hand and then slowly took the seat across from her on one of the plush velvet chairs.

"Randy, can you wait outside please?" Radu asked the large man, who in turn nodded and exited the room. No need for security, the handshake was all he needed to know that this woman posed no threat and that she was going to be offering him something special. He still had some of his old gifts left.

"And what I can do for you Ms. Vorner?" Radu questioned kindly, wanting to appear as harmless as possible, as the woman was cloaked in a dark green aura.

"First, I have to ask if you have any recording devices on your person, anything that can mimic details of this delicate invitation?" Vanessa asked cautiously.

"Not on me, but this place is wired tight. Four cameras are in this room alone. Who the hell knows what else they got in here that I don't know about," Radu responded.

"No worries there. Mr. Leary has the room shut down all to us," she responded with confidence.

"Damn lady, your boss must have some kind of clout," he replied with a chuckle.

"Yeah he has that effect. I won't take too much of your time. I'm sure you want to get to that pretty new wife of yours and those sweet twins," Vanessa started, noticing that her words caused some unease with the wealthy man of wonder. She continued with more caution. "Mr. Leary throws an extravagant party every Halloween for the elite of the elite. This event has been called the greatest spectacle on the planet. The invitation is by spoken word only and can not be shared with anyone. The infraction of spoken word is met with severe consequence. Our team would be honored if you would join us this year and I am here to offer that invitation, an invitation . . ." Vanessa stopped, as Radu stood and approached her rapidly.

She began to stand when he raised a reassuring hand and then placed it over her cotton sweater right on the scar running down her arm. Radu closed his eyes and everything exploded into his gifted mind. Green monsters doing battle with petrified people, fat heads in glorious gowns watching from above and the woman in front of him being sucked under a black surface.

"Well that is really something. Are they masked munchkins or psychos in customs killing each other?" Radu asked as he stepped away and repositioned himself back into the comfortable chair.

"You are the real deal Ricky," Vanessa stated boldly. Fifteen years with mystical monsters had made her desensitized to the fact that other wonders wandered outside of the West Virginian walls. Continuing quickly, "I can assure you that it is real. All of it, the monsters you have always searched for from your books to your short-lived TV series. They exist and you can purchase a front row seat. Only two questions remain. Can you keep a secret, and can you handle the horror?"

"Mrs. Vorner, I can assure you, I can more than handle both. I am in." Radu answered.

The confidence in his voice gave Loch reassurance. She started in on the details and gave him the link to register and make payment. This was a welcomed break from the recruiting process but a shock none the less. New invitations were rare and usually done by the boss himself. Still, a good show, nice diner and night on the town was good for the three companions before the home stretch. This star was an easy pull to snatch from the sky, getting two more to toss in the arena was another tale.

Ricky "Radu" Rabescu tried to sleep comfortably next to his stunning wife in their designer bed, but the images rattled inside his skull. His history played out through dark closed eyes. Supposed to be the fourth abortion of a drunken mother, Ricky survived and was sent to his Bunica in New Orleans at four years of age. His beloved Ronna had the gift and could tell he did as well. By ten Ricky was pulling tricks in the garden district, slyly robbing the tourist of ones and fives with simple slight of hand movements. By thirteen he was using those skills and the gift to pickpocket hardened locals until he robbed the wrong one, or right one has fate would have it. A returning voodoo priest caught the skinny boy before he knew what happened and moments later they were in a bourbon street alley. Expecting a beating, Ricky was beaten with questions and test instead of fist. Once he summoned heat in his palms, the old priest instructed the boy that he would be coming with him back to Dallas.

Starting with parlor palm readings, advancing to spirit cleansing and finally a sold-out show in Vegas, Radu had amassed fame and fortune from his gift. His exotic Eastern European face and mop of curly black hair helped him become the poster boy of the dark arts. Ronna and the priest past before his rise but would always send visions to guide him. The monotony and routine of the show on the strip had diminished his gift, or so he thought. Tonight was the first aura reading and vision he had in years, now his spiritual guides were speaking loud to him. Look at that woman next to you, go lay eyes on the two gifts in their cribs, don't go to this evil event. But he had to. Radu meet many mystics like himself with abilities to sense the future, see into the past and at times control elements. For him, they were all just maybe one step more evolved than everyone else. His true passion was the hunt for ghost, monsters, or anything that may not be from this world. Hundreds of allegedly haunted castles thru Europe, caves thought to harbor creatures in the black rivers of the Amazon and a personal guided tour of Area 51. Radu never found shit. This could be it, the one time he could see real monsters. A final trip, a final treat, before taking his family out of the neon and into a normal world, whatever that is anyway.

15

Salvatore "The Snake" Santini stood alone in the sweltering heat on the veranda enjoying a smoke. He was waiting for his new boss. Sal got the name for being able to slither his way out of any charges.

"You mudahfucka!" Donnie shouted and made pace towards his old friend. They shared a hug and a peck on each cheek.

"What da fuck, soldier boy," Sal replied, looking at Donnie dressed in full tactical garb.

"I know. Big man here told me we was gettin another goombah, but you? Christ, what the hell been going on?" Donnie questioned, ecstatic to see his pal.

"Fuck man, your little night at the opera set off a shitstorm. Been hit and counter ever since. I'll fill ya in later. So what's up wit dis joint?" Sal asked nervously.Da boss said this is the safest place on the planet."

Donnie asked his paisan to follow him and gave The Snake the broad strokes before leading him into the media room where Rex stood, yet again ready to give orientation.

"Shut da fuck up," Sal yelped at the conclusion of what he believed was some tall tale.

"Da truth, I swears. And you're gonna love dis guy over here," Donnie finished by pointing to Rex.

"He's all yours, boss. Take it easy on him, he's slippery," Donnie concluded.

Joy left Donnie as the door closed loudly behind him. This place was perfect for a soldier's hideout like himself, but an underboss? The staff had every book, film, sporting event and TV show available at all time, but news was very limited. He understood and could frankly give a fuck, but some things seeped into the compound. An election result, a terror attack, or something major had a way of finding their ears. If Sal was involved in something one of the cooks or house crew would have told him. Donnie opened his shed for inspection and the thought started to dissipate. Seeing one of his kind just brought back old anxieties, the lifestyle was supposed to be all glamour and glory. The truth was being a major mob player was a twenty-four-hour nightmare, consistently looking behind your back while someone could stab you in your front. Weapons inventory, training and rounding up little green things was a welcomed vacation for the tired tough guy. Five-star food and monthly high-end whores on command was a nice perk as well, not only had Donnie enjoyed his time here, he was thinking about asking to stay. The land of monsters and occasional mayhem beat out any day in the concrete killer jungle. At least in these woods, Donnie knew who the enemy was. Besides, Sal never found out, did he, could he? Nah Donnie thought or he would have been buried years ago.

16

Vanessa started to shiver outside the small pub. Back home was isolated, but Bighorn, Wyoming was literally nowhere U.S.A.. Day four of eighty-degree days and forty-degree nights was taking its toll. Tommy and Vincent headed back to the cheap motel an hour ago with Loch's permission. She was going to wait it out tonight and then off to the Pacific. Her prospect lived in the wilderness and allegedly came to the pub at least every other night unless he was on a hunt or a total bender. Bobby Jo Breech was once considered the greatest North American hunter ever to stalk the continent. Bobby and his brother Billy built an empire in weapons, clothing and eventually the big media contracts that come with big hunt expeditions. The good ole' boys were hero hunters until Billy went all in on everything. Not satisfied with taking Bobby's wife, Billy released Bobby's secret videos. Bobby got his start up money by hunting the most extinct animals in the world on video feed for the elite. Viral footage of his slaughter of a pack of Amur Leopards in Russia quickly made him one of the vilest humans on the planet. Barely escaping mother Russia only to nearly get slaughtered himself at LAX. Two years of international lawsuits later and Bobby lost his brother, wife and fortune. After the miracle of avoiding prison, he isolated in the family's old cabin tucked away from the world. His resume made for the perfect competitor for the gauntlet, but did he even care about money or a second chance Vanessa wondered. If he didn't show up after her next warm whiskey she would never know.

"Ay, fancy pants, he's here!" the white bearded bartender shouted to Loch as she reentered the pub.

Standing ten feet from a dart board, the legendary hunter tossed pointed daggers towards the frame with perfection. He was much smaller in person she thought, TV must add five inches. Vanessa walked over to the old timer at the bar and asked what Bobby drank. Grumpy grandpa handed her a bottle of the stuff she was drinking and two lowball glasses.

Loch took the bottle and glasses and found a table close to the dart board. "Mr. Breech, care to join me?"

Bobby shot a glare at the out of place stranger trying to hide her wealth through a common plaid shirt and basic jeans. Curiosity or maybe hunger for female company got the best of Bobby. He flicked one last bullseye before approaching the attractive stranger.

Whiskey left the bottle slowly filling up the empty glass halfway as Vanessa poured and then slung the drink over to her prey. A liquid snare to catch a big bear. Bobby held the glass past his stubbled face to thin lips and downed the drink like a shot, puffy blood shot eyes peered over the stained glass.

"Another?" Vanessa asked, as the glass was gently slid back to her for another pour.

This time she set herself up one as well before returning the first glass back to her patron. Warm cheap whiskey scolded her throat and sunk into her belly, a welcomed warmth but the aftertaste stuck on the roof of her mouth lingering like an unwelcomed visitor.

Bobby finally spoke. "What ya looking for, lady?"

"You, Bobby. I have a lucrative proposal for you," Vanessa replied. "I work for a very wealthy man and you would have the opportunity to hunt and kill without any interference."

"I already hunt and kill without any interference," Bobby replied.

"Yeah, but I'm confident you have never killed this game before, as well, completion of your hunt would result in a three-million-dollar prize. Participation alone allots you two hundred thousand just for competing." Loch lowered the purse as it seemed three million was like three hundred million in the Wyoming wilderness.

"Are you filming me, lady?" Bobby suspiciously questioned. I don't like cameras."

"No sir, I can assure you that you are not being filmed. As well, the only footage of this hunt is secured for a very elite audience," Vanessa answered back.

"Thanks for the sip," Bobby said as he raised to walk away.

"I can make him pay. I can make them both pay," Vanessa offered. The Breech empire was worth about twenty million now and Lionel could buy, flip and or trash it with four phone calls.

"Can't have either of them killed, bad as they did me, I just can't," Bobby whispered over his shoulder.

"Nothing like that Bobby, we can just take everything that they took from you. Now have another sip and let me fill you in," Vanessa said confidently, smiling as the last card in her deck was played perfectly.

III

MATCH

17

Vanessa walked through the arena at a slow pace with a large bottle of merlot in hand. The first of many traditions she would partake in before the games. Reflections and projections flooded her cloudy mind as the biggest gauntlet ever was a mere four days away. Another year of accomplishments and horrific failures surrounded and adorned the wooded field just as the crimson leaves hung gently from the old oaks. Capturing four big players and fifteen of some of the hardest men she had seen during her tenure had the big man giving her a hero's welcoming when she returned last month. A few days after getting Mr. Breech to sign, Lionel told her to come home and that he had a fifth star ready to shine. Since her arrival, he danced around whom that may be making Vanessa anxious. Knowing the extravagant man, she pondered if it would be a star bigger then the sun itself, perhaps putting them all at risk of exposure.

Entering the lagoon portion of the arena, the place where her legend was born, Vanessa crept to the small sandy beach and plopped down. Staring over the large placid lake, she took a swig of warm wine. Her thoughts turned to some of the new competitors and the odds they faced. Tyrone still had the strength to power through a few waves of attacks but his age and decades of self-abuse would see him fall in the later rounds. The Mountain was fierce and had youth and vigor on his side but he was completely mad. He will probably shine quickly and burn out fast. Bobby Jo would have the best chance, a master of the outdoors, tracking and killing. For sure he must be the odds-on favorite. Sara, what of Sara, Loch thought, as she peered over the watery surface knowing this spot was the best chance her brief lover stood. Could Sara do what Vanessa did years ago? Does she have the fortitude or fight left? Vanessa exhaled and took another longer drink from the green bottle then laid flat on her back.

Staring up at the full October moon, her thoughts drifted toward the staff. Declan was another awful casualty and one that had obviously sent Rex into disillusioned pragmatism. Always a hard man, he had lost any sense of humor or emotion. Both he and his staff showed nothing but astute stares as they carried off their duties to a tee. The two Italians seemed to be enjoying themselves though, an odd pair. Everyone seemed on point but doom seemed to creep through the vast compound like a bad whisper from an old friend.

Probably just the large stakes at hand Vanessa answered to herself as she rose and made way back towards her home. Home? This was all she had known for too long to remember too much of anything else. What lies ahead? Enough money to live like a queen for four lifetimes, but where would she go? Lionel told her she could stay as long as she needed until her plans were made. Traveling the nation was both a gift and a curse, too hot here, too cold there, nowhere seemed likely to live out a utopian existence. Far, yeah at least far away from this place would be essential. The geographic reminders of her time here would be too much of a psychological burden to bear. Love? A Family? Could she start a new life without the nightmares of her past coming back to haunt her or anyone she could start a life with? Loch's head started to swell, not from the bottle she devoured but from the never-ending questions still to be answered.

Flood lights burst open and shot directly onto her silhouette, exacerbating the conundrum in her head. Stumbling from the wine, Vanessa walked thru the dirt road which split the mock old west village. She was impressed, Hollywood itself would be amazed at the detail of the fictious set. Seemingly fitting for the occasion as this year would be the final showdown. Hoping against hope that at least one of her recruits could ride off into the sunset with her come the dawning of November.

Donnie stopped unpacking and made toward the small door of his new room to answer the knock. Security and the whole staff were moved earlier to the small dormitories on the east side of the compound. They traded the lush comfort of the small hotel for the tiny military style rooms to make way for the distinguished guest. Donnie slowly opened the door expecting Rex or one of the senior staff and was surprised to see his old friend.

"Ayyyeee, whatcha up to slick?" Sal questioned behind the cracked door.

"Hey, what's up brother?" Donnie replied.

"Brought a little somethin' for us before the big show," Sal answered, exposing a large bottle of Amaretto. Donnie forced a smile letting the snake slither in.

"Man, Rex would have a fit if he saw dat," Donnie explained, heading back over to his small bed.

"Forget him, that man is zonked out these days. Got any cups?" Sal questioned.

Donnie pointed to the small wooden dresser which housed a stack of plastic cups and some crackers on top. Sal slithered over to the cups and poured the brown sweet nectar to the brims of both cups as Donnie continued his gear check.

"Salute!" Sal toasted, handing Donnie one of the cups and then killing half of his own drink in one gulp. Donnie sipped on his drink holding the plastic cup in his hand cautiously.

"How you think this thing plays out?" Sal asked, now taking a small sip from his drink.

"Man, from what I seen of old contests, we're in for a show. Rumor is they got some tough guys coming in, but once they see those little green fuckers, who knows who will stand and who will fold," Donnie replied.

"And what you gonna do after?" Sal inquired to his old pal.

"Well, I was lined up to skip the pond or head up to Toronto, but I might ask the old man if I can stayyyy heeeeer," Donnie tried to reply, but the words started to slip from his numb tongue. The Dagger's eyes started glazeing over and a grinning foggy snake bent over before him.

"You alright there punk?" Sal spat out before landing an open-handed slap across Donnie's face. Taking both of his hands, Sal grasped Donnie's head and held him up. "Let's see here, didn't mess up that pretty face, did I? Nah, you're still a pretty boy. That's what my daughter thought anyways. All that pussy you got and you had to fuck my baby girl. Ya think I wouldn't know? She was sixteen you sick disgusting fuck! It cost me a fortune to finally get to you, and it was worth every penny to watch these green fuckers tear into you like you tore into her!"

The Dagger fell to the side of the bed as The Snake removed his fangs. Fading quick from the drugged drink, he tried to make a plea but only drool came from his lips. The Snake was going to get his revenge and Lionel had his fifth star.

18

Warm October heat came through the tinted windows of the bus carrying this year's contestants. The arrival and pick up went without a hitch. Ones that had arrived at the airport earlier looked weary and they all looked nervous, but Loch was happy to see everyone in good physical form. She stood as the transport made its way onto the highway and headed toward the compound.

"Thank you all once again for participating. A few things to go through before we arrive. Please keep to yourselves as much as possible, you will have plenty of time to get to know one another once we get settled. Thank you for bringing the bare minimum with you. Should any of you have any phones or devices please pass them forward at once," Vanessa instructed. Several of the nineteen shook their heads, convinced they all followed the preorders perfectly, she started again.

"We should be there in about an hour. I will lead you to your rooms where you can take a brief spell to get settled. Then we have an introduction ceremony followed by a great feast prepared. Any questions?"

More side to side nods followed. Vanessa studied their eyes, nervous yes, but this crew looked focused and prepared. Before returning to her seat, Loch searched for Sara at the end of the bus. The Shark was just staring out the window with a determined look. The greenies are in for a fight, Loch thought to herself and returned to her place at the head of the bus, peering through the large front window as they motored forward.

"You're taking the piss, right?" Rex asked.

"Not at all. You have to realize, Rex, these people hold the keys to the underworld. What we do here is not family friendly public entertainment. My family and theirs go way back. On occasion they do things and get the kind of invaluable information that keeps empires running. I know you took to the boy, but when the old man sends a command, not even I can refuse him," Lionel preached.

"So, besides this complete betrayal, we are going to operate a man down as well?" Rex asked.

"Yeah, well, Sal will be a spectator, so you will be two men down," Lionel replied.

"Fuck, why not give some of the other lads the week off?" Rex clamored.

"Easy mate! I admire you but watch your step. Look old friend, you've done an amazing job. Everything is in place and all you need to do is show the new lot the grounds, stand guard and this time next week you will be humping kangaroos or whatever you do down under," Lionel responded, his joke not breaking the hard man's shocked and angered disposition.

"Can he still win, honestly, tell me he's in with a chance." Rex asked.

"Of course, and I spoke to the old man himself, should he survive the night, Donnie is free to go, or shit, he can stay and with a boat load of money to boot. You like the kid, get him focused and ready, give him a good shot," Lionel answered.

Rex shook his head and stood slowly. Making his way to the glass door exit he turned and looked at the smiling big man, "Keep The Snake away from my pit, Lionel, that's not a threat, it's a promise."

Iron gates parted and the large motor coach made way into the compound. The prison crew's jaws dropped at the luxury estate grounds, while the four former stars barely blinked. It had been awhile for some of them, but they all at one time during their prime had been to compounds such as these. Tyrone thought of his former Motown ex's palace in Anne Arbor and the warm memory allowed a smile to replace the hard mug he wore for the last decade. Bobby Jo thought back to his ranch in Texas and of all the money spent on useless décor that his wife splattered on the expensive walls.

Mike The Mountain was jittery with anticipation, he was the only one let in on the secret of what he would be fighting. Loch had to divulge that to him to seal the deal.

They passed the outer guest hotel and made a quick right down a narrow dirt road, two minutes later pulling up to a modest one-story ranch style building. Everyone scurried out like eager ants up a dirt hill and followed Vanessa to the lobby entrance. Five of the security team stood at attention, assault rifles firmly in hand.

Vanessa smiled again to ease the obvious tension and instructed, "Okay, I will be handing you an envelope with access keys to your private quarters. Please do not share your card with anyone and you can leave them at the desk when you leave the building and pick them up at the allotted slots seen past me at any time you re-enter. We have fresh clothes set aside for all of you. Feel free to wear any of them and please meet back here within a half hour."

Vanessa took the envelopes and passed them to the contestants as they cautiously made their way down the long corridor where rooms ran adjacent to each other. Once inside, the contestants would find comfortable clothes, a fridge full of comfort food and soft drinks, along with a small liquor bar. Keeping them moving and comfortable was always the key to the games. Giving any of them time to think this out would only lead to escape attempts. Once the lobby cleared out Loch took a seat on the large sectional in the middle of the room and exhaled. She exchanged nervous looks with the security guys, lunch and then the horror show would begin.

Rex took the elevator to the basement floor of the main house, he felt shame for the first time in his life. Even as he signed the dotted line nearly a decade ago vowing to warden an evil game of chance, he still felt it was duty and not a moral defamation of his character. This was outrageous. He had many an evening chat with Donnie explaining how things went and how they were both going to leave this place soon. The doors opened and he walked without confidence to the holding cell area at the end of the long hall. No guards at the door as Rex himself designed the inescapable cell. One way in, no way out. Pulling out his phone, Rex pulled up the camera for inside the cell to make sure he wasn't walking into a ambush. Donnie lay sideways on the small cot, his face hidden from the cameras. Feeling secure and checking his pistol, Rex punched in the code and entered the cold steel room.

"Donnie, it's Rex," he started. No response from the former mob prince. Donnie just laid sideways, face staring at the concrete wall. Rex sat on the steel toilet and pondered what to say next. "I had nothing to do with this kid, you know that. But look, there is a way out and I'm damn convinced you can do it." Still no response. "Dammit, Donnie, look at me!" Rex yelped, finally getting the breathing corpse to turnover. Dark bags fell from his eyelids and lines seemed to cut into his brow overnight.

"You know kid, you really look like shit," Rex said, finally getting a chuckle from the doomed dego.

"Thanks. You look pretty shitty too," Donnie replied.

"Son, no reason to trust me, but like I said, please know I had nothing to do with this. Just found out not too long ago and you can get out of this," Rex described with enthusiasm, trying to lift his friend's hope.

"I know, funny. I knew the second I saw his ass here that this or something like this was gonna go down. I fucked up Rex, fucked up bad," Donnie explained.

"Nah, I heard the story, you were nineteen, not much older than her. I seen worse, done worse. You don't deserve this," Rex replied.

"What's gonna happen to me?" Donnie asked.

"Welp, your going in the games, with just a chance to win as any of the other peeps. And son, my money is on you," Rex answered.

"You really think they will let me go if I can make it through the night?" Donnie asked with fleeting hope.

"I do, what happens to you after the games is on you. But if you are still standing at six a.m. November 1st, I guarantee you are leaving this place, guarantee," Rex replied, patting his holstered glock to give visual reassurance to his friend.

Vanessa was pleased to see most of the contestants changing into the nice athletic gear that was placed in their closets. The Mountain of course still wore a satanic homage shirt, too tight, but intimidating enough to send a shiver through a greenie. She led them down a paved path to a picnic area outside the arena. A full buffet was laid out and the group ripped thru the meats, vegetables and fresh fruit. Getting a little more comfortable, some small talk broke out between the group. Most recognized the former heavyweight champion and a few took note of The Mountain, probably more to do with his size than his former gridiron glory. Hungry eyes flew to Sara between bites, Vanessa could read their desires like an open book as well as their confidence rise. If this slender woman could be invited, surely they all stood a chance to win this game and they were told that there could and have been several winners in the past. Lunch concluded and Loch readied the group for the film orientation. This is where emotions run wild as the full details of the game are revealed.

With the security team now fully assembled, minus Rex, Loch led the group toward the media room. Eyes of wonderment clung to the main house's structure as the sheer marvel of the architectural giant bedazzled the contestants. They all entered the media room and took seats per Vanessa's instruction as she introduced the visual orientation.

"It's been a long day already and as always there are more questions then answers. This film will break down the details of your competition. Please keep any questions until the end and once again, thank you for your participation," she concluded and signaled for the start of the video.

Lionel Leary the Sixth appeared on the large screen bigger than life itself. "Hello and welcome to my humble abode. Thank you for your participation in what is considered one the greatest events in the world. In 1863 my forefather came to know one of the great mysteries of the world. Through unfortunate circumstance, he came face to face with a real-life monster. After emerging from a contest with this monster, he hunted and trapped these creatures using them to enrich our family and eventually breeding them as a testament to our family's legacy.

"Through time my family has honored Lionel Leary, first of his name, by throwing a contest such as he was put into upon his brief captivity by Native Americans. Congratulations to all of you for being in the 100th version of this sacred game, as we call it here, The Goblin Gauntlet. Please pay close attention to the following visual instructions and your trainers. We want you to win. We are counting on it."

The introduction from the big man ended and a brief blank screen shone out as the contestants seemed even more baffled from what they just heard. A few gasps came from even the hardest of the group as the participants got their first look at their opponents. The screen filled with quick cuts of Goblins running rampant through the farm. Over the next half an hour all the group were glued to the screen as the calm female voice of the narrator explained the history and rules of the games. Vanessa braced for the ending as the video started to play highlights from previous games, this is where some have attempted to flee in the past as their mortality would be called into question. A couple heavy breaths and oddly a few snickers filled the room, but no one seemed too bothered watching green devils munch through flesh and bone. The video came to the end and lights burst open revealing the groups faces. Loch knew she did well with recruitment, but not expecting this well. This crew looked downright eager. Rex appeared at the top of the sloping center aisle and begun his three day training welcome speech.

"Hello everyone, my name is Rex Taylor and I am here to help you win and survive. Over the next three days, we will learn every inch of your playing field, every weakness of your opponent and every tool that may help you reach fortune and glory. Remember four rules at all times. No fighting with each other and that means at fucking all, nor can you attack a fellow contestant as was explained in the video. You may however work in groups once the games start and I do encourage that. There can be more than one winner and that has happened before. No attempting to escape. Vanessa explained to all of you via your confirmation letters that you are bound to this compound until completion of the games. Your introductory fee's have already been placed in your accounts. Should you try to flee, we will shoot you and you will forfeit your payments. Finally, no attacking or harassing the staff, do that and we will shoot you and you will forfeit your payment. Any questions?" Rex asked. Not even a whisper from the hard crowd. "Outstanding, follow me and let's meet your enemy," Rex concluded and made for the exit leading to the farm.

Several hours after the arrival, Sara stepped out of her room onto the patio and struck up a noose. The

European cigarette gave her an instant head buzz, so this is how the other half lives she thought, enjoying the brilliant mint flavor. The days events ran rampant thru her clouded head and finally rested as she recounted the tour of the farm. Seeing those things on the screen was like watching a bad horror film but seeing them out in the open was another thing. Nasty little fuckers and they looked hungry. Sara saw more than enough horrors in this world, but these things could not have come from this world. Everyone put on a brave face, but she lived in a constant state of fear most of the last ten years and she sensed and smelt it thru the group. Except maybe that big fucker, he really seemed to be enjoying it.

Sara took a seat on the plastic chair that stood idle on the concrete patio and picked up the tablet they were all given. A green screen exploded on the device in reaction to her touch. All the contestants were given one. They could pull up anything they wanted, emails and any form of contacting the outside world were of course blocked, but movies, shows, sporting events and most importantly replays of former games. The bald Aussie had told them the more they studied the creatures the better chance they would all have come game night. Sara fumbled through the options menu; her schedule was laid out as well as what they were told was request night. On the eve of the games they could order anything to eat, drink, or fuck what they wanted within reason. Sara flicked through the menu of flesh. Not a one captured her interest, thinking she would like another scissor lock with Loch. The Shark kept her distance and glances away from Vanessa. Silly to think she actually gave a fuck about her, wondering how many of the other of her fellow participants she had fucked as well. Several loud deep howls broke her speeding train of thought as the forest seemed to come alive in the distance. Not only Goblins, but now we got to deal with fucking werewolves she thought, smirking as she put out her cigarette in the expensive crystal ashtray.

19

Tyrone knelt beside the comfortable bed and crossed his hands on top of the soft comforter, ready to have a morning chat with the almighty. He had seen all manner of evil during his time, some of which sprung from the face he saw in the mirror. What he witnessed yesterday was the reason for his first talk with the lord in many years. How he cursed the heavens during his fall and subsequent life sentence bound to a miserable spell in constant poverty and bad fortune. The little green monsters confirmed for the champ that there was a hell and dammit if there was a hell, then there had to be a heaven.

Tyrone's lips moved slowly as he recited the few prayers that he remembered from his grandmother. He let out a sigh and then took a seat on the large bed to reflect. Maybe too late to save his soul but did he have a chance to walk out of this place infested with vile creatures both animal and human alike? For sure he could still take down two or three of those things, but how many would be let loose in the woods? How many of the other competitors would turn on each other once the going got tough? From a lifetime of betrayal he was betting on all of them to turn.

Another louder sigh exited his round dark lips and he laid flat on the bed to try and steady the speeding train racing through his temple. Meditating as he did during his rise to the title, Tyrone tried to envision a path to victory. Primary training yesterday laid out a few paths to surviving the night. Hiding, he was too large to hide for too long. Group attack, looking into the eyes of his fellow participants showed the old warrior all he needed to know. He was the old man and would be sacrificed quickly when it came down to it. Single combat, try and back into a small space and battle it out all night. Though he trained hard and got his endurance up no way would he be able to go the full six. Opening his now glossy eyes, the champ was ready to accept his fate. A few clear tears ran down the side of his charcoal worn face. His tablet exploded with an alarm. Day two was about to begin and the champ sprung back up into a sitting position with renewed vigor. Rage replaced sorrow, if this was going to be his last bout, then he was going down swinging.

Fresh fall air hit Radu adding to the already fantastic atmosphere of the decorated town of Harpers Ferry. He had come a day early to check out the old

American village. Having been around the world, few other places held the charm of this quaint area. Engulfed in the shadow of the Appalachians, the buildings appeared to be stuck on a slope leading down to the mouth of the Potomac and Shenandoah. Smiling, Radu made his way from the bed and breakfast and navigated a long stone stairway into the heart of the village. Reflecting on the last few months as he descended toward the pubs and shops that hugged the bottom of the stairs. Nothing since that night, no visits from his grandmother, the old voodoo priest, not even a vision since Vanessa gave her invitation. It was almost as if it did not happen. Could his gifts have faded? After touching her and seeing the event he would be attending, Radu was sure this was possibly the real thing. Days after the vision and aura surrounding the women faded like a bad stain washed clean. Reason overcame mysticism over the following months. They must be some kind of cult where little people or mentally deranged teenagers attack the dregs of society. Vanessa had assured him that all of the contestants were lifelong inmates and that no innocent people were hurt or attacked in the competition.

Spending his life in the dark arts did not mean Radu enjoyed violence or death, in fact he loathed it. His gifts just sprung an eternal search for the unknown. The trip was good for him regardless. At the end of the year he was taking his stunning wife and kids and moving to her native home in Portland. She worried that he would be bored once they got there but Radu had enough of the wild life and decades of boredom were just what he was looking forward to. Just one last trip, one last adventure and it was barbeques and ball games. Arriving at the bottom of the steep steps, Radu headed right to check out the impressive bridge and have a look at the house where John Brown raided many moons ago.

It was morning but the overcast dark clouds gave the impression of late afternoon. Few others walked the streets and the town was covered in head to toe decorations for the Halloween season. The first flash hit Radu suddenly. A scarecrow across the road hung at the front of a bookshop, seemingly turning from pale straw to green and blood dripped thru its buttoned eyes. A few quick blinks and Radu removed the vision from his own eyes. Now keeping his sights in front of him another apparition appeared. Several stores hung evil faced carved pumpkins from their awnings. The orange sliced faces blinked green as Radu passed each one. With a quickened pace he made his way past the shops and stood before the civil war historical house. Taking a deep breath, Radu approached the metal sign and read of the raid on the home. After taking in some brief history the mystic made his way to the concrete barrier which overlooked the ancient rivers. Tiny waves crashed below the two bridges that hung above and dark clouds rose from the angry water below, a perfect fall portrait played out in real time.

Several minutes passed and Radu was ready for an early lunch. He turned and began to make way toward one of the small pubs when a group of young students came from behind ready to take in the majestic view he just admired. As they hurried by him, each of their faces began to shift from excited children to green horrific monsters. One by one the green devils seemed to run at Radu. Quickly making his way past the horde of multi faced monsters he found a bench at the side of the barrier. Radu rested his mind and closed his eyes. A few seconds later he nervously reopened them and glanced back out at the crowd. Just smiling children and teachers taking pictures, no little green monsters, no frightening faces. A few moments passed and the man of magic rose to get something to eat. Chalking up the visions to exhaustion and anticipation of the event. He passed the historical armory house again on his way. The small building was home to one of the largest raids in American history, little did Radu know, there was to be another one to come not far away.

Rex was pleased to see everyone on time and eager at the entrance of the playing arena. Donnie was transferred during the night to the contestants building. Rex saw to the transfer himself; he gave Donnie more words of encouragement, advice and a stern warning to not try and escape nor mingle too much with the rest of the participants. With his squad in place Rex began training day two.

"Good morning everyone, hope you are all rested and ready. Today we are going to tour the arena, learn about the weapons you may use and have a tactical session with some of the green bastards. Feel free to ask any and all questions as we go through the sessions. Please remember that what you learn today can and will make the difference between walking out of here wealthy or being carried out dead," Rex concluded.

Determined faces shot back stares of concentration and anticipation. The Aussie knew he had some warriors in this lot, under different circumstances any one of them could be under his command instead of following it. Rex started the tour thruuogh the entry gates and lead the group to the weapons table. Knives, crossbows, axes and other weapons of the wilderness were spread over the large wooden set piece. The long-haired man who sliced up four was particularly thrilled at the selection of swords. Rex had a briefing on all of the contestants and had an inkling this fierce fencer would be slicing up his fair share of green meat. Instruction was given that everyone could pick one weapon as they entered the arena, but that other weapons would be spread out thru the playing field and can be used at any time. For the first time in the games firearms would be placed in the arena. Revolvers could be found in the old west section but the Aussie warned that though pre-loaded they could jam and try to stick to more conventional and tested weapons in a fight. The group surveyed and toyed with the weapons for a while. Most went for the knives and large axes. Sara picked up the crossbow and quickly put it down, the weight of the weapon was too much of a burden and she started fumbling with lighter swords and knives. After the group seemed satisfied with their options Rex began to lead them on a tour of the arena.

The arena was broken into four sectors this year. The miles long deep forest seemed to intimidate the group as it appeared to never end until they reached the stone courtyard. Small stone and granite houses decorated this area along with columns and statues.

"It's a nice break from the dark woods, but those woods will be lit up by floodlights during the contest so this is at times a good place to rest or put your back up against something to avoid attack from behind. They can climb and cut down trees but the little fucks have trouble getting up stone and concrete," Rex explained.

GOBLINS

A few more miles of woods cut between the courtyard and the lagoon sector of the arena. Rex instructed one of his staff to head out to the small island in the center of the man-made lake to demonstrate how deep it was. The lake itself was two hundred yards in circumference, goes down to eight feet deep, and has a six-foot grassy island in the center. The Goblins do not swim well but they come in green waves at anyone inside the water and the cold October air turns the lake icy in the middle of the night. Only one person has won the games by staying in the lagoon all night. After the aquatic demonstration they all headed to the final sector in the back of the arena. The old west playing grounds were new and sure to attract the older attendees of the games to this area. Five dusty buildings stared out at each other over a dirt road. Rex asked everyone to take their time and have a look inside the buildings and the area. The group broke up taking a tour of the tiny town. Darting between the saloon, whorehouse and other caricature old west settings, they all looked for the best places to hold up and or pose an attack. After the grounds were covered, Rex lead the group back to the farm where they were introduced to their opponents a day earlier. Passing the barn houses and home of the glamours the warrior entourage settled in at the fighting pits. Rex took off his gear and went into the center.

"You will have your weapons with you for most or all of the time, but should you get disarmed, note that these things can be taken apart by hand," Rex explained.

A giant horn rang out and a greenie charged the Aussie. Rex quickly blocked a weak punch and wrapped his hands around the green devil's neck. Holding the smaller Goblin by the throat, he continued his lecture. "Going for the throat is good, even the little lady can crack their windpipe with a good squeeze, leaving them with no air to breath.

"They have week knees as well and one stomp can put one of these bastards down," Rex exemplified by bringing his boot down on the Goblin's interior kneecap, crushing it in the process. The Goblin screeched and fell to the ground as Rex released his death grip.

"Now, one blow you want to avoid is to their melon heads," he continued by striking the monster with a hard blow to the side of its cranium, exemplifying the hard shell that wraps around their tiny brains.

Snickers and a few applauses came from the crowd. Rex caught Donnie's eyes. Donnie knew that the Goblins being thrown out here were no more than a year old and basically teenagers. The exercise was to instill confidence into the contestants and prevent any escape attempts or suicides, both of which have happened over the years. Another hour passed and Rex concluded the day's training, sending the contestants back to their building for a great meal and rest. He reminded them to study the tablet instructional videos and to come up with an effective strategy. They were welcomed to train and exercise in the late afternoon but tomorrow would be an early day. The final day of training was reserved for survival skills, medical training and a detailed break down of how the game would be played out.

Most of the group headed to their rooms after the smorgasbord was finished, some went to the front area outside to exercise but Bobby Jo went to the back side of the building and climbed up to the roof top. A guard gave him a passing look. The nearest fence was a mile away from the building and charged to take down a pack of rhinos. Bobby Jo had been dead silent since the trip in. A master hunter observes and does not react until time for the kill. He studied his fellow participants, studied the creatures, studied the staff. Those who roamed in the building below him would fall within two hours he thought. The creatures could be tracked, hunted and killed with relative ease. Bobby Jo worried about the staff though. All the talk about wanting them to win was lip service, he had heard it all before. Tomorrow they would get an actual game summary on how the contest is played out. Bobby Jo knew that there would be more to what they were going to tell them. He knew hunters, he knew killers and just about everyone on that bus with him could take down one or two of those little green fucks with ease. Ahead of the game as always, the master stood roaming the roof. He studied the walled bridge that flowed through the arena. If they tried to fuck him, Bobby Jo would find a way to get up on one of those and take out a few of them with him.

20

Radu awoke in a frantic flurry, his sheets soaked from sweat. Quickly rising from the nightmare, he hurried across to the window and attempted to open it with force. On the second attempt he got the old heavy wood latch to give and flung the stained glass skyward. Cool fall air rushed into the room, a welcomed relief to the personal inferno he was slumbering in. Radu's visions through the night were horrific. Bodies being torn apart by green devils, ear shattering wailing filling the West Virginian sky and blood-soaked trees were just a few images that filled the mystics resting head. What had his skin leaking sweat were the visits from the old voodoo priest. Warning after warning an old creole cut through the images like a sick commercial break interrupting a fright film. His mentor's skin turned from light brown to bright green as he cautioned of impending doom.

All of the night's horrors replayed in Radu's head, causing him to start to hyperventilate. A couple of deep inhales of fresh air settled his nerves and cooled his heated olive skin. Reason settled over madness as

Radu made his way to the bathroom eager for a hot shower. Slowly the old pipes kicked into gear and water flowed out with surprisingly strong pressure, quickly fogging up the room. The warm water washed away the rest of Radu's anxiety as he started to ponder the long day's events. Instinct more so than his talents had kept his path fairly clean thru the years. Navigating good and bad deals and avoiding the pitfalls of celebrity were due more to his calming rational thinking than his gifts. Both reason and mysticism were calling for him to exit the shower, the town and the state as soon as he dried off. Should he leave? Could he leave?

Not concerned about getting his invitation fee back, which was considerable, but very concerned about his host willingness to let someone stand them up on date night with access to their dirty little secret. After drying off, Radu plunked down on the edge of the large country bed and peered at the old radio clock on the counter. Almost noon, he had an hour to either make his escape or suck it up and play out the night. Both options rattled around his skull under the thick wet mop of coal black hair. Radu rose and went to the one closet in the room, he grabbed a heavy designer shirt instead of the hooded pull over that hung next to it. Gazing into the oak mirror a smile finally broke across his face. He was going to go, one last exotic dance before the eternal ballet of boredom began.

Rex was impressed. No he was damned impressed. The contestants thrived beyond all expectations he thought to himself as he led the caravan of golf carts back to the contestants quarters. Knowing that they were all either killers or highly trained athletes of high caliber, the Aussie expected all of them to thrive at the physical and weapons training early on. What he did not expect was the level of concentration and adaption to the outdoor survival training. They all asked the right questions and studied his instruction with vigor, giving off large amounts of confidence that they were all going to be walking out come November's arrival. Most knew how to hide and scavenge, but their knowledge of tactical combat and group assaults galvanized the former high-ranking commander. Hoots and hollers broke up his admiration trip as the line of carts rounded the bend and started toward the outside of their temporary flats.

Spread through the front of the building were large kegs of ale and a feast fit for a king. What had the men of the group shouting was the line of good looking young women sitting on plastic chairs behind the large tables. Rex hid a smile, knowing that if any of them should last the night, their first trip after the games would be to the compound doctor to get a really painful shot to the cock. Extending his large right arm, Rex signaled the carts behind him to stop as he circled around to face the group. Slowly rising from the cart, he peered over the group and began.

"Alright animals, your feast awaits you. Before you began let us go over some things, so you all are prepared for tomorrow night. Everything behind me that you lot have ordered is all yours for the night. Of course, several of my team will be here to supervise and or replenish any of your desires. You can drink your fill, but you are going to want a clear head tomorrow night, so know your limits. We assemble at three in the afternoon tomorrow to prep. You have access to your companions and all the food and drink until four a.m. this morning. We are too late in the game to replace any of you, so know if you play the fool, start fighting with each other, or are dumb enough to try and take off, you will be darted and placed at the head of the games tomorrow for a quick exit."

The smiling faces Rex spoke to turned sour quickly, but the point was made. After signaling to release the horny herd, Rex got back into the cart and took off to prepare for the night's more distinguished guest. More hoots and hollers erupted as most of the contestants sprinted toward the lovely ladies, most of them having not been with a woman in years.

Radu climbed up the step of the bus and took a seat up front. Only a few other guests of the games had stood outside the bus station with him. All dressed in proper clothes, the few vagabonds that accompanied them at the stop looked confused at their attire. The returning guest of the games knew protocol and were admitted to be dropped off at the estate while their teams awaited in the town's hotels nearby. New guest, like Radu, had to meet at a simple bus station and be brought in. A final inspection, Radu thought to himself as he was scanned by a large man before entering the bus, handing his cell phone to him as well. No devices of any sort were words splattered all over the final invitation he received months earlier.

Open road cut to dark woods as the bus ascended the mountainside, a few minutes later pulling up to a massive brick wall and huge steel gate. Once through the gate, Radu admired the compound. When he finally became a name in Vegas, the wonder kid was brought to Mr. Newton's palace. Until today he had never seen anything like it. The Lionel estate was engulfed in gorgeous perfectly maintained woods and stunning stone architecture. Pulling around to the main house was most impressive. An enormous fountain structure stood in the middle of the paved circle which greeted guest to the front of the towering home. More like a large private luxury hotel in Europe, Radu thought to himself, quickly forgetting the previous night's horrors and taking in the architectural marvel. Gliding away from the main house, the bus slowed as it approached a two-story motel style building.

Outside, more nicely dressed people mingled. White, black, brown, and yellow people dressed to the hilt laughed and smiled, looking more like a United Nations fundraiser than a group about to celebrate a slaughter. A large man dressed for war handed Radu his one bag of luggage and nodded toward the front door of the building. Guests of the games smiled and waved to the newbies as they entered. Being a worldly man, Radu was shocked to see some familiar faces in the lounge are. Two famous politicians and actress Michelle Pare were among the temporary residents of the place. Standing by the large front desk area was the man himself. One of the biggest men Radu had ever seen, Mr. Leary did wear his weight well in the custom made dark black suit that was loosely painted over his massive frame. The new guest halted as Mr. Leary began his welcoming speech.

"Hello and thank all of you for attending my family's iconic fall event. I am sure most of you are eager to indulge in the festivities but once you get to your rooms, please take some time to rest up and get acclimated. I have such wonders to show you."

A small applause broke out and the new guest started their way to the front desk. After receiving his key card, Radu made way to his room on the second floor. The place was nice, but nothing he had not seen from any four star in Vegas. Once inside his room and unpacked, Radu had a look at the agenda sheet on the small table resting next to his nice king-sized bed. A tour of the grounds started in about an hour, then dinner and entertainment. The building would have open breakfast and lunch buffet on Halloween. All guest were to report to the main house by ten p.m. that same night. The back of the one sheet had a map of their area with guidelines and time frames for where they could and could not go. What struck Radu as odd was next to the word entertainment and in parenthesis was the words "options beyond your belief." He could believe a lot, but curiosity overcame reason as his mind ran wild thinking of what wonders this place held.

By late evening most of the contestants were in a fuck fest but four remained at the tables outside. Sara, Donnie, Bobbi Jo, and Tyrone tried to throw down some food, but their already overfull stomachs resisted. All but Donnie sipped on good imported beer, Donnie had a glass of good red.

"So where exactly did you come from good looking?" Bobbi started.

"Jersey," Donnie replied.

"No shit. I mean you showed up here a day late and barely said a word during training. You didn't even glance at any of the girls and I know of the champ and super swimmer. Now you're too pretty to be a prison boy, so once again where did you come from?" Bobbi inquired.

"I'm Donnie and I'm just layin low and restin' till the games begin," Donnie answered.

Donnie thought about divulging it all, who he was, what he was doing here, and what they were all about to get into. He took a large swig of the delicious sweet wine and started to tell a tale when he felt a soft touch on his shoulder, a woman's touch. Expecting one of the whores to be trying to lure him in for a romp, he was shocked to see The Shark standing over him.

"You two can have a piss off later, but Donnie is it? Would you please walk me to my room? It's not safe for a girl to walk alone with drunk, horny, criminals running around in there," Sara requested.

Donnie nodded, took her slender hand in his and they made way to her room. Tyrone let a laugh escape and stood to end his night as well.

Radu did his best to keep a calm demeanor as he entered the dining hall at the main house. A life spent in the dark arts and he had never seen anything close to what he saw during the tour of the grounds. After the long hike along the stone bridge that surrounded the arena, the guests were taken into what Mr. Leary's team called the farm. At first, Radu trusted his initial perception of these games as the clumsy Goblins stumbled around too far to make out. They simply had to be in costumes. Once they got to the fighting pits and the scary looking Aussie put on a display, Radu knew this was for real. He did it, he finally seen a real monster. They were horrific and terrific. Nasty fucks with odd bodies and misshaped heads, but their hair almost made them human. Boy do they not like humans though. They charged the Aussie and one of his team ready to rip their heads off. After a few go's, the guests were treated to a display of Goblin filth. Once the pit area was secure, the host threw rancid meat in the middle of the large dirt ring and let some beasts loose. Obviously starved judging from their thin bodies, the Goblins ripped into each other and the ones still standing devoured the meat. Tails in the air, chomping all the way through the bone with their daggered teeth.

The replay of the day's events came to an abrupt halt as fellow guests introduced themselves and several of them recognized the famous mystic. Radu was happy with his table, a bunch of older Americans. Though he could converse in a few languages, the thought of not being able to understand his table mates would only have added to his increasing anxiety. A stunning waitress handed him a leather-bound menu. He scrolled over the first page which was surprisingly simple for the extravagant event. Meats, pasta and fish entrees accompanied with soup or salad beginners. The second page was written in neon green and the word Goblin prefaced each of the same courses. Noticing his inquisitive appearance, the old bearded gentlemen next to Radu leaned in to share a secret.

"It's exactly what it is young man. I highly suggest the Goblin stew and Goblin porterhouse."

Radu forced a smile and nodded to the man who looked like an old sea captain. Feeling a vile surge about to erupt from his stomach the magic man quickly threw down some water. The liquid calmed his tummy and cooled his heated throat. After ordering from the non-Goblin side of the menu, Radu sat quietly, taking in the banter from the table. Most of the conversation was of their children and families, as per typical of the elite, they loved to talk about all of the accomplishments of their kin. Everyone there was about to be a paying part of a human slaughter and all they could do was talk over each other about how Madison or Phillip were trotting the globe, making absurd money, by essentially doing nothing. Money makes money, Radu thought to himself, was one of the first things his accountant told him when he reached seven figure heaven.

His thoughts turned to his twin boys. Could he ever tell them about what their father attended as a willing paying participant? The appetizers arrived before he could dwell on the sad thought. After the meal, most of which Radu stared at his food hoping not to get a glimpse of someone digging into green meat, the lights dimmed and Mr. Leary stood. The ringleader addressed his carnival of wealthy freaks.

"I hope everyone enjoyed your meals, I see most of you newbies were too yella to eat some green." Laughter erupted through the gaudy dining hall, by the high-pitched tone of it, most were already well past half sauced.

Lionel continued, "Your tablets will be to all of you shortly. Please turn them in before you leave to return to your building. Everyone will get them back before the games begin tomorrow. You may use your set accounts for biding and purchases or see Vanessa now to switch codes for any other account you may want to switch to. Thank you again for being part of our Centennial celebration!"

This must be the entertainment portion of the evening, Radu pondered to himself as the waitress returned to hand tablets to each person at the table.

One finger touch and the screen popped open. Several simple headers filled the screen with simple options, eat, drink, fuck, drugs and glamour. Radu quickly found out that you could pretty much order just about anything from those options for your in-room entertainment for the evening. From pure heroin to a woman that looked young enough to get a twenty-year sentence. When Radu hit the glamour button out of curiosity, just a blank screen with numbers appeared. He turned to the captain next to him.

"What's this for?' Radu asked, pointing to the glamour screen. A big smile parted the old man's beard.

"You're about to find out son, once again, you need to try it," the old man responded.

On que the lights in the room dimmed and the room filled with applause. Radu noticed the long head table had been cleared out and now there was just an ordinary stage area that sat just slightly higher than the rest of the room. Bad dance music poured into the room from speakers hidden somewhere in the ceiling. Radu skidded his seat back in fright when he saw the green thing come out on to the stage unattended and then slumped in wonder as the Goblin became more visible. Cheers came from the crowd as the glamour made her way to the center of the stage. Stark naked, the Goblin spun and danced for the crowd. The female turned and bent over, raising her tail to reveal her pretty pink parts. Radu had been to every shady strip club north of the strip. After watching a pregnant stripper piss on a customer, he thought he had seen it all. But this was next level shit.

Heat rose in his palms and he quickly diverted his eyes to the tablet. A running bid was on the left side of the glamour section. One hundred fifty thousand and rising every second. It did not hit him for a moment as he was trying to cool his elemental hands, but then yes, you could actually fuck one of these things. Feeling comfortable enough after a brief mental break, his eyes returned to the stage. Red curly hair rolled down to the gorgeous green thing's perfect ass. It was pouring red wine down its front, going from the neck, down two huge tits, and dripping from its Goblin lady parts. But it was the tail that got Radu's palms heating up again, the tail swaying back and forth was the sexiest thing he had every seen. Never had one of his gifts acted like this without his control, but never had he been turned on by a naked monster before either. His tablet lite up and a thunderous cheer exploded to the table next to him. Someone had won the company of the creature for the night. Thinking that was the last of it, the music kicked back up again and another dime piece demon walked on to the stage. Radu quickly made for the restroom, he needed a quick reprieve before he set the tablecloth on fire.

"Ya mind?" Sara asked.

"Nah, fuck can I bum one too," Donnie responded.

Both had torn into each other as soon as they entered the room, a deep dagger into silky shark meat.

"So, like the hillbilly asked, who da hell are you?" Sara started her interrogation.

Donnie laughed and choked on his lit up cig. "Man, you did all that just to find out who I am?"

"Well I probably would have fucked you anyway, but yeah everyone's been eyeing you up since you arrived late. I just thought maybe you missed your plane or something," Sara explained.

As much as he enjoyed The Shark, he could not divulge everything. The Snake could even get to a shark and he was instructed to keep his cards close to his chest. He would feed her some bait but not let her chomp on the whole truth.

"Well, I fucked up. I fucked up bad and this place is either my way to get out of trouble or end up where some think I belong," Donnie explained, hoping this would satisfy her inquisition.

"I thought that Italians were great liars. It's

no wonder you got busted for whatever," The Shark responded, not satisfied with his explanation.

"Really doesn't matter how I got here does it? We are all going into a death match tomorrow," Donnie said, trying to put an end to the cross examination.

Sara took a long drag and started in again. "I saw how you and the bald man interacted with each other and some of the other goon soldiers. You hardly put any effort in at training and seemed to know every inch of this hell hole. I'm just looking for an advantage if you got anything. If not, you can head out after you butt out."

Convinced she was not on the take for some kind of special advantage, Donnie did what he had taken an oath not to do many years ago, The Dagger ratted. Sara was enamored with his tale, from the Albanian legendary hit to his time here at the compound and the venomous bite from the snake. When he finished, she was laying on his stomach facing him, her cold blue eyes showing empathy for his plight.

She shifted her head down and rubbed his side, "I'm so sorry that happened to you, but do we have any chance of making it out in one piece?"

"Well there have been a lot of winners in the past and you are a world class swimmer. I would try to mock Vanessa's road to victory," Donnie responded.

"What road to victory?" Sara asked.

"Didn't you watch Vanessa's highlights from the games?" Donnie asked.

"Nah, watching all those people get chewed da fuck up was depressing. What did she do to win?" Sara responded with vigorous curiosity for the information on her crush.

Donnie patted Sara on the head and sat up to light up another smoke. "The Legend of Loch Nessa. Vanessa Vorner was once a meth princess. Her daddy was the biggest meth dealer in the east. Their little drug palace was not too far from here. When federal agents started sniffing around, Lionel asked them kindly to fuck off and move. Well the good ole boys told him to fuck off. Meth daddy had a small army and half the town to back him up. Bout a year later, Lionel's men lead fifty Goblins to the meth palace and let them loose. To the hillbillies' credit, they took down the Goblins, but after the slaughter there was only a dozen of the meth king's men left and Lionel's trained guard took them apart quick. He brought the meth king back here and had him hung to a tree to watch his only child Vanessa in the games.

Vanessa had been swimming in the rivers before she could walk and she would hide loads of merchandise in the rough waters where only a strong swimmer like her could get to. During the games, she got cut early before she could make it to the lagoon. Bleeding and afraid, she tread water and fought off one Goblin after another for six hours. At the end of the games, she was the only one left. Lionel and the crowd fell in love with her, she was asked to stay on for a period of a few years as to make sure she wouldn't run to the law and from that day on she was crowned Loch Nessa, Queen of the Sea."

"Damn, six hours of treading and fighting. I'm not so sure I can last that long in freezing ass water!" Sara exclaimed.

"It's your best chance to try and stay around the island. They don't swim well and once the water goes over their heads, they panic. Just maybe try and wait out the first few hours because that water is freezing and you could go numb quick," Donnie instructed.

"Yeah, or fuck it, I might just go knives blazing like I've done my whole life. By the way, what happened to her daddy?" Sara asked.

"Lionel gave Vanessa a choice. Feed him to the Goblins or she had to chop his head off herself. So, she chopped her daddy's head off and Lionel had it spiked on the veranda for a year. He's a sick fuck, Sara, and I would like to tell you that we could roll in bed another day, but who the hell knows what these people got in store for us tomorrow night," Donnie explained.

"In that case," Sara responded crawling her way on top of The Dagger leaning in for one last sharp kiss.

21

Small rays of light peeked through the cloudy West Virginian sky and heated the top of Rex's bald head. Just hitting ten a.m. and he was already weary from the day's work. Ten of his best and himself met the Japanese on the shore of the Shenandoah five hours ago. How they were going to get those boats thru the shallow canals was their problem. His was only to get the cargo to them in one piece and knocked out enough to endure the hour-long journey into the Atlantic. Rex wiped his brow and took aim, shooting another dart into a greenie.

The team had done a good job so far. Forty were drugged and he wanted another thirty done before the afternoon. Rex was nervous as Lionel said not to worry about Gobzillas and that he would handle the release of the big one. Most of the greenies were lured out of the barns by the fresh meat laid through the front of the porches, but many, almost sensing the trap, were cowering behind closed doors. Population had grown too rapid for his liking and the foreigners only wanted one hundred to ship and all of the glamours. Last greenie count ended at two hundred and four. Too many for the Aussie's liking, but he was confident the contestants would take out a lot. In fact, he pondered if they would come close to making the boss nervous by taking down a hundred. The Sixth seemed unconcerned when this was brought up at the final briefing the night before. This year's group was the fiercest, most focused lot he had ever encountered. Not my problem he thought to himself as he loaded another dart. A red sprinted toward a leg of deer and tumbled quickly as the dart pierced its neck. Rex exhaled and cracked his stiff neck, peering at the cloudy sky. He was ready for the pure sun of the Sydney coast.

Vanessa was shockingly delighted to witness the enthusiasm amongst her recruits. Confidence rang through the air as they sat down for a late lunch and filled themselves with the fatty fish, pasta and fruits laid out before them. All great foods for energy. They all had the option to take the adrenaline shot before the start of the games, all but Bobbi Jo accepted. Glancing at her watch, which showed four p.m., Loch began her speech.

"Thank you all for your fantastic participation so far. Never in the history of these games have I been so confident that each and every one of you have a great chance at walking out of here tomorrow alive and wealthy beyond your dreams. When you finish your meal please take the next few hours to yourselves either in your rooms or around the building. The weather will be brisk tonight, so I recommend getting some rest and much needed indoor heat before being exposed to the elements. Please be ready to assemble at ten p.m., at which point we will have an inspection. You will be able to select your primary weapon and then sent into the arena. Remember that a small arsenal of weapons will be available throughout the grounds but please select the weapon you are most comfortable with. You may go anywhere in the arena at any time, please avoid climbing as always, these little bastards can climb and chop very quickly. Do not pin yourselves down. Should you take to the water please know that even though the temperature may be at forty degrees, the average swimmer will reach exhaustion and slight hypothermia at around forty-five minutes. Any questions so far?"

The group nodded side to side, apart from one. Bobbi Jo stood and spoke. "So six a.m. comes and there are still monsters in the midst. What happens then?"

"They will be terminated on the spot," Vanessa answered quickly and sternly.

No more questions arose from the confident crew. Satisfied, Vanessa headed to a cart and made her way back to the main house. She threw one last glance to

Sara and gave a reassuring smile. The Shark smiled back but the first signs of accepting her mortality shone from her crystal clear blue eyes.

Radu exited the motor coach with the rest of the esteemed guest, figuring walking the quarter mile to the main house was beneath his fellow attendees. The vast hall greeted the mystic with grandeur. Bronze Goblin statues were stationed thru the long hallway leading to an enormous great room past them. A serving staff that looked like they were pulled off a Milan runway offered perfectly looking cut hors d'oeuvres and sparkling champagne. A massive full bar sat to the left, filled with exotic looking bottles. Radu wanted to keep a clear head but made way to the bar looking for a cool drink to calm his heated body. The visions and rising inferno inside him had subsided but the uncertainty of the night made him anxious. He got a cold draft beer and the cool ale numbed his tongue and his nerves. After a quick glance around at the aristocratic crowd Radu felt shame for the first time even after a life of trickery, this seemed so wrong. They were about to watch and cheer as human life was hunted for sport and entertainment. Another large chug settled his pacing mind and he went for another drink. One or two more before the games began, he contemplated, staying alert was important but a little buzz may go a long way to bear witness to the slaughter to come.

Sara and Donnie approached the weapons table. Donnie was happy to see the fixation dagger still on the block and grabbed it quickly. Sara examined the swords.

"Use the long light one. It has more reach and a strike below their necks makes them bleed like soft pigs," Donnie explained.

They went over tactics and had another romp after lunch. She was happy that they were going in as a team, the others had not posed a threat to her, but it would be a different game in the deep dark woods. They were the last two to make their selections as the big Aussie waited patiently. Once they stepped away from the weapons table Rex began his tactical tirade.

"Never and I mean never, in the history of this competition have I ever felt so confident that each and every one of you can last the night. Remember your training, work together and rest when you can. The night is long and coming to kill you. Will you lie down and die without a fight?"

"No!" the contestants responded in a strong and confident unison.

"Will you let a lavish life slip from your dead fingers?" Rex shouted loudly.

Once again and with rising voices the group responded, "No!"

"Didn't fucking think so. Now get out there and chop those fuckers up," Rex finished.

A roar came from the amped up group and they hurried into the carts. As they pulled away full of piss and vinegar Rex pondered for the first time, what if all of them survive? Would the big man allow such a spectacle or be willing to part with that much money? The last cart disappeared into the dark woods and he made his way back to the tower to unleash the beast.

Vanessa radioed in Rex to get ready for the horn as the big man stood next to her ready to dump his lungs into the old piece. With the exception of last year's debacle, she had always been confident that the games would go off without a hitch. This year was the first time she actually felt panic and empathy. Never had she cared much for the contestants, dregs of society that they were, but this group was different. She prayed for either quick deaths or victory for her favorites. Lionel bellowed into the horn, followed by thunderous cheers that rose from those who stayed at the veranda near the opening gates hoping to catch the first glimpse of the creatures in action. Most of the crowd headed out over the bridges, tablets in hand, to their favorite spots. The Japanese contingent would be accompanying them along with The Snake in Lionel's private seating area.

The giant gate opened and everyone leaned over the side to get a good look at the first wave. Vanessa joined them as something caught her eye on the giant screen set up for the V.I.P. crowd. The Mountain was at the front of the gate, ready to meet the green demons head on. The crazy bastard was chanting in Latin holding an enormous ax. Ten greenies charged the giant man from the jump, a few of them stopped to chomp on the loaded meat sitting at the front of the gate. Unbeknownst to Rex's crew, Lionel had that meat laced with pure cocaine to amp up the monsters. Mike The Mountain Mouldon fought with the fury of Lucifer in his soul, quickly chopping down the first three Goblins to reach him. His powerful swing taking their heads off with ease. For the first time Vanessa saw fear in a few of the creature's eyes and she enjoyed it, not as much as the cheering crowd who were going crazy for the big man.

"Release the next ten," Lionel told Vanessa, with a bit of worry on his face. Clearly, she did her job well.

Vanessa signaled in and a laughing Rex gave the signal. The Mountain fought back and forth with the couple of greenies brave enough to take him on. He had his hands around the throat of a blonde one and bite into its neck, letting the demon blood pour into his mouth. Gasp of disgust erupted from the crowd. About to take on the other two with confidence, The Mountain finally took a step back. Ten new amped up greenies charged the giant man and poured over him like a dirty green wave. Mike made a few heroic efforts to push them off but the force of the group effort was too much and the Goblins had a satanic steak for dinner.

After the insane start to the games, Radu found the contest rather boring as he took up position in the middle of the wooded section, suggested by the old man at dinner. A cat and mouse game ensued as the Goblins were finding it hard to locate the contestants. Hour two brought about the next big conflict as a dozen Goblins finally cornered a large group of men right below Radu's position. Guest started running toward the area for a perfect peek. The Goblin horde had found some weapons and were good with the old bow and arrows. Filled with muscles, tattoos, and courage, the men charged the green attack. Flashing swords and large knives split open soft green flesh. A few of the monster's arrows found their mark and put four of the humans down. Radu gazed with wonder but was surprised how much this looked like a fantasy movie from another realm instead of real life, until the screams started. The surviving humans took back off into the dark woods as the Goblins started to feast on flesh. Screams ripped through the quiet air and Radu had to turn his back and try to block out the cries with mental fortitude. He made his way past the gathering crowd, the sight of the slaughter did not affect him, the death wails very much did.

Halfway through the night Tyrone thanked the Lord for his good fortune as he holed up on the second floor of the stone house in the courtyard. Three a.m. shot back from the digital watch all of the contestants were given before being sent into the night. The champ heard a few screams and some scattering below, but was yet to encounter a greenie. While training he was told some that survived the games were able to hide the entire night. Tyrone felt the monsters would be more dangerous out in the open, so he took refuge in the courtyard.

Noticing the one building with a second floor upon his tour of the grounds, the large man felt that hunkering in the small space would give him the best chance to ward off any attack. He was approached several times to partner up, but a lifetime spent with criminals gave him the knowledge that it would be each man for himself when the cards were down. Snarling sounds below the stone steps interrupted his quiet meditation. They were here. The champ rose with his large knife in hand. A red caught the human scent and charged the steps, slipping on the unfamiliar stone surface. Tyrone took advantage and pounced on the creature, bringing his knife into its neck. Yellow and red blood poured from the Goblin and sprayed over the white stone walls. Tyrone tossed the thing down the steps and saw that a few other green fucks were waiting to charge. They looked at their fallen brother and seemed boggled as how to approach the large black warrior. One at a time they crept up the stone stairs. Tyrone stood atop the steps swinging the blade keeping them at bay.

The champ began to tire after a few minutes and took a few steps back. He turned and looked to the window, that was his exit strategy. Only about four feet to the small awning to the first floor and another five to the ground. As he backed towards his exit the first Goblin sprinted up the stairs towards him. Tyrone got a slash to the side of the monster's face, but the creature was able to knock the knife free with a whip of its tail. Now face to face, the champ raised his real weapons. Throwing a straight right cross the champ shattered the large green nose and the counter left hook dislocated the small green jaw of the Goblin. Staggering for a second and then tumbling to the ground, Tyrone The Terrible just recorded his forty third knockout. Tyrone felt the sensation that he had during his first one, until he glanced up. Three more Goblins made their way to the top of the stairs, grinning with pointed hideous teeth.

"Come on motherfuckers!" The champ shouted, ready for round two.

He turned back the clock and threw furious combinations. The blows shattered teeth and bones, but he was fading. After receiving blows individually, the three came at him in unison and wrapped around his massive upper body. The force of their charge sent all four through the window, bouncing off the stone awning and landing on the hard concrete ground. The champ went down for the count as the fall cracked his head nearly in two.

Radu wandered alone around the stone bridges pretending to watch his tablet and show vague interest, really not wanting to ever hear those screams again. He found his way to the old west sector of the games where a crowd of guest seemed to be enthralled. Against better judgement, he peered over the wall at the ongoing battle. The swordsmen from Texas was slicing green fillets with relative ease and playing to the crowd. Four of the nastiest Goblins Radu had seen surrounded the warrior. They came all at once, tails raised. He danced a perfect death waltz stepping between them like a ballet dancer and taking off their limbs like a ruthless executioner. Once again, the vision looked like an old western showdown instead of real life. Enjoying himself, the Texan gave a little bow to the crowd once his opponents laid split in pieces on the dirt road.

Once again not the sight of the slaughter, but another sound sent chills through Radu's spine and caused his hands to radiate. This sound was of no ordinary Goblin, but something bellowing from the depths of hell itself. Shuffling at the end of the makeshift town towards the showmen swordsmen was a gigantic Goblin. At least nine feet tall and built like a Marvel studio super villain. The thing let out another gigantic roar and charged the celebrated hero below. The Texan's face changed from confident man to scared little boy in an instant. With barely a second to maneuver or flee, the giant Goblin reached the man and with one chomp took of his head with a big bite. The only screams this time came from the onlooking crowd as they backed away from the edge of the bridge. Radu guessed they were twenty-five feet above the surface, but if this thing could climb or jump with force, they might be next on the menu. Two brave contestants came guns blazing out of the saloon building and shot at the monster with old six shooters. The bullets knocked it back but barely took effect. They tried to flee out of the old west town and into the woods, but the giant Goblin was as quick as it was big and caught them quickly. With one hand on each of their necks, the massive monster held them up like rag dolls and smashed their heads together. The crack of their skulls was another sound Radu could have lived without hearing. After snacking on the two corpses for a bit, the green giant took off back towards the other end of the town center, toward the lagoon. Frightened and invigorated, the crowd followed the same path.

Donnie and Sara cowered behind an old large maple as a few Goblins approached and sniffed the air. Donnie knew they had caught their scent. He quickly glanced at his watch, four a.m., two more hours till freedom. They had both been lucky through the night. Sticking to the perimeter as Donnie had suggested, the current from the electric fences seemed to keep the greenies away. They were smarter than their mongoloid features suggested. Only coming in contact with a few single creatures thru the night, which Donnie disposed of quickly with his skill with the blade. Sara found out quick why they called him The Dagger. A few became several real fast as the small red-haired monsters let out a yelp. Seven in total started making their way toward the two.

"Two hours left, make for the water, get deep, you can ride this out," Donnie instructed The Shark.

"The fuck are you gonna do?" Sara questioned.

"I'll head south along the fence, I can get by them, just get through the clearing and hit the water, whatever you do don't stop till your in the deep near the little island," Donnie answered.

Sara grabbed his chiseled chin and wrapped her lips around his, then took off toward the water. All of the Goblins heads turned toward the commotion. Donnie stood and gave a shout, then took off in the other direction. He had a good thirty yards on them before they came at him. Planning on making it to the old west town, he stopped dead as the sound of chopper blades pierced the sky. Goblin and human alike gazed at the sky. Sara made it to the lagoon quickly and plunged in headfirst. The cold water numbed her frame, but she had swum in colder during training before. Quickly, she made her way to the island and grabbed the outer grassy edge to pull herself to the surface. Thru wet, stringy, blonde hair, Sara saw that none of the greenies had followed her. A quick sense of relief was drowned out by the giant spotlight above. A chopper was lowering something below into the water. Something big, something green, something angry.

Donnie made it to the lagoon and let out a scream for Sara. "Come back this way!"

He listened to Rex talk about the giant Goblin, but the Aussie's description did not do justice to the thing that was being dropped into the lagoon. Dropped from the chopper, the second giant entered the games with a thunderous splash. Donnie started to make for the shoreline when he heard the nasty snarling behind him. Backing into the shallow water, the Italian made his stand. Donnie made surgical cuts to the creatures as they came at him. Perfect fatal incisions to soft green flesh, spilling squirting mucky blood into the dark water. He glanced back to see Sara making a dash toward him. No sign of the giant. Donnie found some space and started to sprint around the edge in attempt to meet Sara at the other end. He led the three remaining Goblins into the shallow end of the water slowing them down.

"Keep to the right!" Donnie shouted, as Sara's head went side to side above the surface.

Finally getting forty yards from the three green assailants, he turned to see where his aquatic angel was. Sara soared from the sea like an ancient siren, still in perfect forward stroke position. Donnie's shriek shattered the sky. Sara's midsection was engulfed in the giant Goblin's mouth, its clawed hands wrapped around her head and ankles. In one motion, the giant beast bit down and pulled, ripping her in two. A whizzing sound flew past Donnie's ears as he stood stunned in the shallow water. Without comprehension, he saw all three goblins fall into the dark water not ten yards from him. The last one he saw had an arrow through it's eye.

"Run you fucking idiot!" Bobbi Jo shouted, as he sprinted to the right of Donnie and back into the woods.

Vanessa fought back emerging tears as she watched The Shark get chewed in half, her phone blowing up.

"Put him on," Rex demanded.

"Lionel, Rex is on for you," Vanessa explained, offering the big man the phone as he cheered with the rest of the soulless crowd.

"I'm busy, tell him ring me after," Lionel responded, brushing off the call. Before she could respond to the Aussie, he told Vanessa, "I herd him. I'm coming over."

She pressed the red symbol and hung up, quickly thinking of an exit strategy. This was going to get ugly. The Asians had dropped the second giant in the games and no one knew that was coming, especially the head of security. What else was the big man planning? Just over an hour left and four total contestants remained with fourteen greenies and two giants roaming the arena.

Bobbi Jo and Donnie, made it to a secluded section, and finally held up for a breath. "Jesus fucking Christ, what the hell was that thing?" Bobbi asked, panting like a hungry dog.

"A big ass fucking Goblin. Man, thanks for bailing me out there," Donnie answered, his entire being filled with emotion. Anger, fear, sadness and fury poured through his olive skin.

GOBLINS

"Why the fuck didn't they tell us about them and how the fuck do we take one down?" Bobbi started to question, his eyes started to flutter, and the words slurred out of his dry mouth.

Donnie went to him and held him up against a tree before he slumped over. The Dagger gave his hero a quick one over, the back of the master hunter was soaked in blood. A deep claw wound poured dark red blood down his back.

"Ran into a few an hour ago, got four of em' then a little bitch jumped me from behind. Got her claws in me before I could flip her. But I took the cunt's eyes," Bobbi explained, showing his green and red thumbs to exemplify his removal of the Goblin girl's spectacles.

"It's not that bad. Under an hour to go," Donnie said, trying to console the man that saved his life, tearing off his sleeves to try and patch the deep wounds.

"Nah boy, I'm done, ain't no cloth gonna stop this river of blood, it's my time," Bobbi preached, as he started to fade.

"You wanna give these fuckers a real damn show?" Donnie asked.

Bobbi Jo coughed out a laugh. He saw the look in Donnie's eyes. He saw that look in the mirror the day his brother took his life from him. It was the look of revenge.

Rex approached the brass of the games and shouted, "The fuck is going on Lionel?"

His old Asian counterparts rose and blocked off the Aussie's path. Rex threw a quick head butt and split one the Asian's nose open.

"Enough!" Lionel shouted loudly, as two Japanese guardsmen drew their weapons.

"What is this madness, Lionel?" Rex questioned, with steel determination and fury firing from his eyes.

Lionel made toward the side glass door, signaling Rex to follow. Tempers cooled and everyone went back to watching the conclusion of the games.

"Are you fucking mad, son?" Lionel questioned.

"Me? Two giants in the arena and how many Goblins have you released tonight? Sixty by my count," Rex answered.

"Remember boy, this is my house not yours. You can stand down and go out with pride or get set down and go out in a bag," Lionel responded.

Rex heard the footsteps behind him. He turned and saw the ugly British fuck pointing a nice Ruger at his head.

"Now fuck off," Lionel instructed. Reason took over emotion and Rex headed back to his post.

"Sorry gentlemen, just a little mix up. Please refill your glasses and enjoy the conclusion," Lionel politely demanded. He turned to Vanessa and motioned for her. "So, chrome dome is a little emotional. Let's see how he likes this. Hand me your arena map tablet," the boss commanded.

Lionel took the tablet and pulled up the gate holding area. With three taps of his fat fingers, thirty goblins were released into the arena. He handed the tablet back to Vanessa and smiled. She nodded and slowly made her way to the small kitchen behind their section of the veranda. Staff flew by her, arms full of food and liquor as she grasped the granite top of the kitchen island and took a breath. Lionel was sick in the head, but this was another level of madness. Four lives had a great chance to make it through the last half hour and he releases thirty more starving monsters into the games. What else did he have planned? Was anyone safe? Was she safe? Vanessa grabbed a glass off one of the staff's treys as they passed and downed the drink. Quickly spitting it back up, gin, she fucking hated gin. She closed her eyes and took a deep breath, exhaling slowly. Loch Nessa regained her perfect posture and strode back into the cooling fall night, with a plan in place.

The wop and the hillbilly made it to the tower unnoticed. From the cheers and screams coming just to the east, they both knew a final battle was brewing. It was, as thirty-six goblins and one giant surrounded the last two convicts in a fight against time. Donnie sent a quick prayer up that they die quickly.

"Damn, I don't see him," Donnie explained.

He was expecting Rex at the tower overlooking the gates. He was going to give the good man a chance to escape before delving out his master plan. He punched in the code, happy to see it worked and the steel entrance door slid open.

"You sure you can make this climb?" Donnie asked, he had plugged Bobbi's wounds with leaves and packed them with dirt, slowing the pouring of blood.

"Damn right. I'm gonna catch you on the flip side," Bobbi answered.

Donnie watched him slowly climb the wide ladder to make sure he could make it and that Rex was not holed up in the control room. Once Bobbi got to the top, he made way to the release center. Everything Donnie said was right. A giant screen showed the holding pens. They were white, which meant they were all open. Then he looked for the main gate to the farm and found it with ease. Punching in the simple numeric code, the perimeter went from red to white, he had just unleashed the entire farm. Walking back to the ladder as life started to eek from his body, Bobbi leaned down and gave Donnie a thumbs up. Donnie shouted something to him before his eyes gave one last blink.

Bobbi tumbled forward and his body bounced twice off the side walls and landed five feet from Donnie at the base. The ultimate hunter had finally fallen.

The Dagger exhaled and took off quick, wanting to beat the green storm coming. His watch started beeping, six a.m., he had made it. Stopping for just a moment, he contemplated victorious surrender. He could take his revenge in the years to come. Closing his eyes, he saw Sara ripped in two, Bobbi tumble, and The Snake smiling. Dismissing the crown, he took off toward the main house. Arriving quickly, he was met with floodlights and loud applause. The Sixth was grabbing for a megaphone to announce the champion. Donnie tossed his dagger with perfect accuracy at the esteemed guest, hitting the snake right in his stomach as he stood four feet from the big man himself. Before the first screams were heard, Donnie lifted Bobbi's crossbow and put another perfect shot in The Snake's throat. The Dagger heard the spray of bullets follow his quick footsteps.

Arriving at his final stop, Donnie aimed the arrows at the control box beyond the entry fence and hit it with destined accuracy. He quickly reloaded and shot another, hitting the mark again. A fire shot up his back before he could get off a third shot and he fell to his knees. Watching the fence swing open and hearing the green horde approaching let Donnie die with a smile on his face. More bullets flew from above and Vincent, who slept through the last hour guarding the front fence, popped a couple into his old coworker's lifeless head.

Donnie's plan played to perfection as a green cloud passed through the entrance of the arena. Vincent hardly had time to comprehend what Donnie was doing before the first Goblins sprinted through the entrance. He got a few shots off before they swarmed him like bees on honey. The Goblins from the games were quickly joined by the ones in the farm and made their way through the compound, crazed and starving. The two Giants made swipes at the guests above.

Lionel made his retreat to his room after the Japs told him deal off and took to their choppers. Rex smiled, hidden at the end of the bridge as he watched The Snake get split in two and tumble over the wall. He signaled to his team a code orange, which meant get the fuck out of Dodge quick. Once the boss took off to his safe room, Vanessa dashed towards the front door, satisfied that the monsters would be feasting on the guests for a hot minute, allowing her to escape. She was correct. Most of the guests had not done a full sprint in decades and the Goblins made their way to the crowd quickly, scurrying up to the bridge with reckless abandon. The vast majority were pinned and had to head back into the arena sections of the bridge becoming sitting flesh ducks. Goblins howled at the full Halloween moon as they overtook the soft humans in a blood bath.

Radu was walking back to the entrance, more interested in getting home than watching the conclusion when he saw everyone running back toward him. Slowly, the ones in the back started to fall like duckpins getting hit by a green ball. Screams and snarls ripped through the air. Several, no dozens of green creatures of the night tore thru fancy slacks and elegant dresses, painting their black attire red. A few made it past him, ready to follow, he stopped and embraced the horror. He deserved this, problem is if you chase the devil long enough, you find him. Radu closed eyes and pictured his wife and kids as the first beast knocked him to the ground. Seconds later a few more snacked on his sweet skin, death came fast as the mystic floated towards his grandmother.

The Asians made it to their choppers untouched. Six glamours quietly awaited them as they were to be flown directly to the ship in the Atlantic. Looking sweet and innocent the boss man ordered three be put in with him and the others put down. His three guards, one still reeling from Rex's blow, pointed their pistols at the green models. The gorgeous Goblins wicked smiles gave away their attack, and two were put down quickly. The other four attacked. Before the three gunmen could reposition, they were being death humped. Clawing and biting thru the human flesh invigorated the sexy beasts. Pilots from the choppers signaled for their bosses to get in and when they knew they were not going to make, all three took off. The last of the bosses cursed his abandoning crew from his knees, a slick soft green rope flung around his neck. With a hard twist the glamour Goblin snapped his saggy old neck with her tantalizing tail.

Inside the main house a few dozen Goblins caught the guests that were near the entrance of the house when the slaughter began. Red mist sprayed over expensive white furniture. Shrieks of pain from the humans echoed thru the great halls along with what could be described as laughter from the monsters. Fitzgerald attempted to go out as a proper Englishmen as he took one of the swords from the wall and meet his fate head on. A sprinting Goblin knocked the sword from him right away and head dove into his crotch biting off his cock. Not the heroic exit that Fitzy imagined.

Rex was happy to hear the retreating quick-fire gunshots, confident most of his crew would make it out. He enacted code Orange only after he saw the giants. Fearing the boss man had finally lost his mind, he needed an exit plan for the boys. He pressed the code to the big man's front door and it slid open without hesitation, the dumb fat fuck did not have the foresight to have an emergency code put in. Rex crept in from the side expecting to maybe get in a fire fight. Lionel was pretty handy with a gun. Nothing should have shocked him at this point but seeing the fat man pounding one of his whores was insane. His whole world just fell apart and he still needed pussy. How that girl was breathing was a whole other thing that defied reason.

"Oye big boy, give the lass a break," Rex shouted, trying to contain his laughter.

"You fuck, don't you give up?" Lionel questioned, rolling over dripping sweat like a mutant pig.

Rex motioned for the girl to get out and came around slowly to the side of the bed. "For fuck sake, really? A fucking revolt and you come up for a roll around, you are one mad sick fuck," Rex preached.

"You're just too damn serious, I've told you that day one, got to enjoy life," Lionel responded, and then pulled his pappy's pistol from under the pillow and placed a perfect shot.

A red circle appeared and expanded on Rex's peach bald head before he fell. Lionel's laughter was cut short by the screams in the hall. He rolled his fat naked ass to the edge of the bed and trotted to his front door. Getting pumped by a four hundred pound man was bad, but by the look on the girl's face, not as bad as having your tummy clawed open by the sharp talons of a Goblin. She staggered toward Lionel and he stepped aside as she fell and bled out. Before he could seal the door the first creature crept into the room. Lionel fired two bullseyes into its thick green melon. Hurrying to the panel he heard the multiple scraping of sharp claw footed nails against fine marble. The fucking Aussie set the elevator on automatic Lionel thunderously recognized. His sweating fat fingers would not register on the touch screen and two of his pets came to see daddy. Lionel fired three last frantic shots, only one hitting a greenie in the arm as they pounced on papa. Four more showed up quickly and the six Goblin children ate The Sixth of his name.

Vanessa finally took a rest on a large stone. Once Lionel took off, she knew it was time to split. All of the cars were locked in the garages so she had to take to foot. Once upon a time Vanessa knew these woods and could run around blindfolded, only the roar of the falls let her know she was just north of the town. Another two-mile jog and she could contact her man at the casino to hold up and see how it all played out. Vanessa knew it would get bad one day, but not this bad.

Sunlight started to break the horizon over the Shenandoah and the legendary sea star went to the edge taking in the view. How something this beautiful could look over a world so ugly made no sense, but nothing made any sense did it, she pondered. A burst of gunfire broke her reflection. Not far away by the sound of it and the burst sounded like the automatics Rex's men used. Human screams followed along with the victory cries of them. Before she could plan a route out, several Goblins broke from behind the trees and started a sprint towards the compound queen. Flesh and blood dripped from their sharp teeth. Reds, how she hated the reds. Vanessa was not even fond of red headed humans, yet alone monsters. She lived as a privileged slave her whole life, slave to her father, slave to The Sixth. She was going out on her own terms. Vanessa waited until she knew they couldn't slow down and took off for the edge of the cliff. Smiling as she plummeted to her end with the cool West Virginian air and four shocked Goblins at her back, Vanessa hit the water with fatal force and sunk to the bottom of the Shenandoah. A perfect final resting place for a siren of the sea.

22

"Got damn motha fucking little shits," Ole Willy shouted to no one in particular. Large puddles of vomit greeted the old man as he entered the railroad station. Pricks can't handle their shine, he thought to himself. Willy knew there was going to be a big clean up after the Halloween festival, but to see and smell the vomit first thing set him off. Still cussing he made his way to the back utility closet to grab the mop and bucket. It was Sunday, but he wanted the place shining before the pricks from Amtrak came in on Monday. The assholes would call the township and complain if the place were a mess and he was sure they wanted to replace him with damn Mexicans.

Willy spotted two red boots coming from behind the last bench at the end of the station. "Jesus Christ, Billy. You get all fucked up too, ya bum. I told yer ass you can't be passing out in here!"

Only a soft chewing sound responded to Willy's shouts. Spotting something wet as he approached the end row, Willy was primed to go off on his friend thinking he pissed all over the floor also. About to unleash on the red booted man, his words got caught in his sagging old neck and only a muffled yelp squeaked through his mouth. Blood, not water poured all around Billy as a Goblin sat on his fat chest, snacking on his throat through a mangled grey beard. Willy turned and went for the exit at an impressive pace for a man of his age. Just as he reached the last step before the open parking lot, the Goblin pounced on his back. Willy twisted and turned as the creature started to puncture his chest with blows from it's clawed hands. Accidentally falling backwards, Willy had the little green bastard pinned behind him. He found his voice and screamed for help into the early morning deserted town. Willy quickly looked for any kind of weapon to fight this little fucker off until he could make the fifty yards or so back to one of the shops.

His broom lay a few feet away and would have to do. Whatever this thing was, it was not that strong, and the old man felt he could fend it off. Willy leaned forward and flung his body back with force, a final blow to phase the monster in an effort to buy some time. Unfortunately, Willy's head connected with the Goblin's melon and sent a searing pain through his skull. Still following the plan, he sprung up and made for the broom as he started to wobble. Just as Willy got hold of the broom, a searing pain ripped through his calf. The Goblin sunk it's teeth into the old man's thin leg and was chopping away. Woozy and tired,

Willy turned with the broom and with the last bit of force he had, brought down the handle right through the ugly fucker's eye. The Goblin yelped in pain and let go of his leg frantically reaching for it's injured eye. Willy started to take off towards the shops.

After a few steps he hobbled to a slow walk, never looking back to check on his green assailant. Losing blood from the leg wound and still reeling from the head shot, Willy grabbed the old post at the end of the parking lot and took a moment to recover. Looking back toward the scene of his assault, the green bastard had fled and was gone. Turning back toward the open road, all the color fled from his face. Peering up to the old bridge about thirty of his attacker's buddies were making their way toward the town. The sight of the green horde shocked him into action. Willy went straight for the safety of the old buildings knowing he could bust in any of those doors with ease and get to a phone. After two steps towards his rescue mission, Willy felt another sharp pain, this time in his chest. Bad time to have that heart attack he thought at first before glancing down and seeing the arrow sticking in his sternum. Willy quickly fell to his knees and brought his head up. Old brick head was sprinting toward him, bow in hand, and mouth full of exposed razors. Right before the Goblin got to it's snack, Willy raised his hand and gave the green bastard the middle finger.

Also available from Lance W. Reedinger ~

CLAWS

Thirty years ago, the dark heart of the Chesapeake Bay swallowed an innocent soul. The sea spit out an abomination hell bent on revenge. Beaten back into the bay that night, the beast slumbered for three decades. This October, those unknowingly linked to that night bring the beast back.

Lance W. Reedinger presents the world's very first Were Crab tale.

Available for purchase on Amazon.com and Boutique41publishing.org.

GOBLINS